"So—in a roundabout way, you're saying yes?"

Rick Jablonski seemed amused as Marissa gulped, thinking she must be mad. Marry this man—tie herself to him for life?

"What's bothering you, Marissa?" His smile was slow and assured. She avoided his eyes, looking down at the table.

"There is something, but I hardly know how to put it," she began, and Rick interrupted with a short laugh.

"Directly is usually the best way," he advised. "You're unlikely to shock or offend me with a sensible question, so shoot from the hip."

She drew a deep breath, but in spite of his advice, she didn't find it easy.

"The marriage . . . is it to be purely a business arrangement? In name only? Or had you planned on our really being man and wife?"

Lee Stafford was born and educated in Sheffield where she worked as a secretary and in public relations. Her husband is in hospital catering management. They live in Sussex with their two teenage daughters.

Books by Lee Stafford

HARLEQUIN ROMANCE
2963—YESTERDAY'S ENEMY
3048—A SONG IN THE WILDERNESS

A PERFECT MARRIAGE

Lee Stafford

Harlequin Books

TORONTO • NEW YORK • LONDON
AMSTERDAM • PARIS • SYDNEY • HAMBURG
STOCKHOLM • ATHENS • TOKYO • MILAN

Original hardcover edition published in 1989
by Mills & Boon Limited

ISBN 0-373-03088-6

Harlequin Romance first edition November 1990

CHAPTER ONE

MARISSA was out close to the northern boundary when she saw him. A tall, craggily built man with a long, easy stride, he was strolling along, looking observantly about him, taking in all he saw, with no hint of furtiveness or unease, but as if he had every right to be there.

She had walked quickly and angrily from the house, with Idris, the black and white sheepdog, at her heels, so wound up from her latest confrontation with Vicky that she was, until now, unaware of the distance she had covered. She badly needed to be alone, and here was this stranger, this…this intruder, who had no business on someone else's property, and who was, moreover, invading her solitude.

She stood and watched him approach. Idris's flank quivered against her thigh, and her hand rested on the top of his alert head, but the man came on unconcernedly, pausing only when he was within a few feet of girl and dog. He wore casual trousers and jacket, but Marissa, whose business it was to know about clothes, recognised the stamp of a good tailor and fine tweed. Certainly he did not look like any of the scruffy old poachers or inexperienced ramblers who had lost their way, who were part of the landowners' lot, but he was trespassing, nevertheless.

All the pent-up irritation and near-despair Vicky

had aroused in Marissa came to a head as she faced this unwelcome interloper. Since somewhere deep down she knew he was not really the cause of her anger, she tried to maintain a reasonable courtesy in her voice, but in her present mood she was incapable of injecting any warmth had she wanted to.

'Excuse me,' she said coolly, 'but do you know you're on our land?'

'Is that a fact?' The soft drawl betrayed that he was an American, which did not disturb Marissa, who had visited the States several times, and had a number of American friends. But she did not care for his tone, which was ever so slightly patronising, or the go-away-and-play-little-girl smile which accompanied it. 'And who might "we" be?

Marissa's coolness spilled over into a frozen rage. He was questioning her right to ask him to leave land which had been her family's for more generations than she could count.

'"We" are my father, Davis Beaumont, and myself,' she replied glacially. 'I should point out that there's no footpath or right of way across the land on this part of the estate. Perhaps you've lost your way?'

He actually chuckled, a low, throaty sound which made Marissa's scalp tingle inexplicably with a prescience of danger. They were far away from the house, or from any other habitation, and he could easily be some sort of weirdo, she realised.

'Lady, I never lose my way,' he remarked casually. 'I'm always exactly where I intend being.'

Marissa did not scare easily, but he was a big man, powerfully if leanly built, and she, although tall, was slender and, right now, far from strong. She was suddenly glad of the warm canine presence beside her, but oddly enough, Idris, although his ears were pricked interestedly, was not even growling. He did not feel threatened.

'You're trespassing, whether by intent or by mistake,' she said, putting on as fearless a front as she could achieve, as if some exacting photographer had snapped out, 'Give me more bravado!' 'If you don't leave, I shall be obliged to set the dog on you.'

In order to present this authoritative image, she had to look him straight in the eye, and the face which looked imperturbably back at her was intriguing rather than conventionally handsome. A long, aware, intelligent face with furrows of experience creasing a broad brow and firm jaw, strongly defined eyebrows arched arrogantly over eyes that were coldly blue, with a hint of green somewhere in their depths, like the sea when a storm was brewing.

He glanced at Idris, and his broad shoulders rose and fell in an easy shrug.

'What, him?' he said, with dismissive amusement. 'Dogs usually like me, actually, and I don't think he'd harm me unless I were foolish enough to attack you.' He gave his thigh a light slap, and Marissa felt the friendly thwack of Idris's tail against her own leg. She did not know whether to be reassured or annoyed. Dogs generally had a sure instinct of whom to trust, so she presumed she was in no real physical danger. On the other hand, she had been neatly divested of her only authority, since this person did not seem prepared to accept hers.

She said, 'All right, if that's the way you want it.

I'm going back to the house now, and you'd better be gone before I get back with my father's shotgun.'

She knew the pounds had dropped from a frame that was whip-slim to begin with, but the full knowledge of her frailness only came to her as those blue-green eyes appraised the long, slender body in blue jeans and a baggy sweater which emphasised its lightness, the hand resting on the dog's head, so translucently thin that the fine blue veins were traceable.

'I should think the recoil would probably kill you,' he observed, and what angered her most was that it was not said unkindly, but with a light touch of compassion.

'I suppose I'd better put you out of your misery. I'm not a trespasser—in fact, I have your father's express permission to look over this land as much and as often as I choose.'

Marissa frowned, puzzled.

'I don't understand. Why should he allow you to do that? Are you a friend of his?' she asked doubtfully, fairly sure that he was not. She knew most of her father's circle. Unless, she thought, chilled, this was one of Vicky's hangers-on. But no—she had to admit, this man looked altogether too decisive, too purposeful, nowhere near lightweight enough for Vicky.

He smiled, but she was far from reassured, because there was a stalking, predatory quality to this man's humour which made her feel exposed and uncertain, like a hunted quarry unable to find camouflage. And his next words turned her limbs to ice.

'Not exactly,' he said. 'But it's usual to view a property thoroughly before buying it. Wouldn't you agree?'

It was a long time before she was capable of replying. Or at least, so it seemed to Marissa, whose tongue was locked into that same cold, fossilised immobility as the rest of her body. Only her mind was still active, racing, clicking feverishly from thought to thought.

Finally she said, with a leaden, desperate insistence, 'You must be mistaken. Grafton Court is not for sale—not to you or anyone else. You can take my word for it.'

The strange American ran a large, capable-fingered hand through close-cut, springily waving fair hair, and quite irrelevantly it occurred to Marissa that his was the kind of head one sometimes saw on Roman coins…some buccaneering general who had made it to Emperor.

'I guess there's a communication problem in your household,' he said. 'You should talk to your father.'

But he's avoided me resolutely since I arrived home two days ago, Marissa thought. We've never actually finished any conversation we started. There was always something he had to do, somewhere he had to go…and suddenly, horribly, she knew that it was true, what she had learned with such unexpected awfulness from this man she had met by chance. It explained so much…her father's almost guilty evasiveness, Vicky's cocksure smugness, bursting to tell what she had clearly been instructed to keep quiet about.

She could scarcely see the stranger's face through the mist in front of her own eyes. Tears of angry denial and despair were threatening to blind her, but she'd be damned if she would allow him to see them! Talk to your father, indeed!

'That's exactly what I'm about to do!' she said
thickly, spinning around and setting off at a fast trot
which quickly made her breathless.

'Hey! Wait a minute!' She heard the American's
voice call sharply after her, but she didn't stop. The
effort of running was making all her ribs ache, and
her legs felt as if they were about to buckle under
her. Her breath came in great, forced gasps, and
there was a throbbing in her temples . . . her whole
body was telling her that she could not take this
kind of physical punishment, not yet. But she
stumbled on, until she knew he would no longer be
able to see her, and then collapsed in the welcome
privacy of a thick copse, the last thing she
remembered, Idris's rough, wet tongue licking her
hot, dry cheeks.

And when she next awoke, she wasn't in the
wood at all, but in bed, in her own familiar bedroom
at Grafton Court, the home she had loved from
childhood . . . as had so many of her ancestors
before her.

Memory came back to Marissa slowly, bit by
painful bit. She had been in East Africa, modelling
swimsuits and cruise-wear against a background of
lush scrubland and native villages, when she had
gone down suddenly with a tick-borne disease,
which had turned out to be more serious than
anyone anticipated. The next thing she knew, she
was being flown home by air ambulance. Modern
medicine had quickly countered the infection, but
the illness had left her weakened and debilitated,
and the doctors insisted it would be some time
before she was fit to work again.

Marissa knew they were not joking—the few tentative steps from her bed to the chair next to the window left her gasping with exhaustion, and she knew better than they did how strenuous a model's day really was. Besides, she thought ruefully, staring at her reflection in the mirror, while slimness was essential, no one really wanted emaciation—those hollowed-out cheeks, that lacklustre skin—ugh!

'Is there anywhere you could go to convalesce for a month or so, at least?' the friendly young registrar had asked, smiling at her as if he would have liked to take her away and nurse her personally back to health. For even now he could see that Marissa was beautiful, the streamlined, thoroughbred body, the perfect bone-structure, unimpaired by illness, the long, cloudy tendrils of night-dark hair curling gently over her shoulders.

She hesitated. Whilst she had been ill, she had refused to let anyone know about it at home, insisting to herself that she would be up and about in a few days, and there was no need to fuss. But, like an injured animal, she knew there was only one place where she could begin to feel whole again. She had to go home. Vicky would be there, of course…oh, well, bother Vicky! Grafton Court was *her* home, where she belonged.

'My father lives in Herefordshire,' she said. 'I could go there.'

'Splendid—all that fresh country air will be just the job!' the doctor agreed.

And so Marissa caught the InterCity to Newport, then changed to the little train that chugged through the ravishing, melancholy beauty of the Welsh borders, past the familiar sugar-loaf mountain at

Abergavenny, running alongside the broad River Wye until it parted company with it to pull into the station at Hereford.

The cathedral bells were pealing—it must have been a practice night—and the spring evening was just shading into dusk. Marissa would have liked to catch the country bus that meandered through all the small villages and hamlets, picking up and depositing shoppers and farmers' wives, all of whom appeared to know one another, and gossiped mercilessly about the last person to get off. But it was too late; the last bus would have left town an hour earlier, and anyhow, she was desperately tired, and needed to get home as quickly as possible, so she hired a taxi.

Darkness was closing on the peaceful Herefordshire countryside, but it was still light enough for Marissa to see the acres of fruit trees just ready to burst into blossom, the hops tied picturesquely to their long poles, the first crop of new lambs in the fields. She blinked away glad tears, wondering, as she leaned back against the upholstered seat of the car, how she had ever endured leaving all this.

When she was younger, it had never occurred to her that she would do so. Vaguely, she had supposed she would marry some local landowner's son or well-set-up young farmer, and they would live happily at Grafton Court, bringing up their children and riding their horses, looking after the land as it looked after them.

She became increasingly aware as she grew up that all was not too healthy in the financial department. Things broke at Grafton Court and were not replaced or repaired, essential maintenance wasn't always carried out.

But she didn't want a lot, materially—only what was always there, and had been as long as she could remember—the changing seasons and the unchanging land, the fecund red soil, the sleepy villages and the soft, slow, lilting voices of the local people who had known her since she was a child. And surely things could not be that bad? Her father still enjoyed his cigars, his brandy, and his visits to the races.

Then, when she was seventeen, she had come home from boarding school for the last time, ready and eager to be Davis Beaumont's hostess and helpmeet, the châtelaine of Grafton Court, when a cute little pocket Venus with Delft-blue eyes and sugar-blonde curls had unrolled herself from one corner of the ancient, comfortable sofa in the room they had always called the 'Hall'.

'*Cariad*,' Davis Beaumont had greeted her, like the cat which had just stolen the cream, 'I want you to meet someone very special to me. This is Vicky, and I hope you and she are going to be the best of friends.'

Marissa, then, had been as tall as she was now, but without the poise and assurance her later training had given her, she seemed all arms, legs and gawkiness, whereas the young woman confronting her was neat and compact as a doll, completely together and sure of herself.

'My,' said the pocket Venus, looking up at her as if considering an immense height, 'what a great girl you are!'

Marissa knew then, with an awful sinking of her heart, that Vicky would never be, and had no true desire to be, her friend. Not that she was openly unkind or unpleasant to her; indeed, she was all sweetness and charm when Davis was present. But she had ways of excluding Marissa, of cutting her out and making her feel that she was very definitely *de trop*. Vicky wanted to be part of a couple, she did not want a stepdaughter only five years younger than herself cluttering up the place and making demands of any kind upon her man's attention.

At seventeen, Marissa did not have the weapons to fight this determined seductress. Boarding school had educated her and given her a little polish, but basically she was still a shy country girl who was happiest in her own company and that of the few who knew her best, who loved to ride for hours alone across the fields, at one with trees and streams and wildlife. Vicky made her feel inferior, too, with her petite blonde prettiness, because she had not yet realised that she possessed a rarer, more striking beauty.

Besides which, Davis Beaumont was utterly besotted with the young woman who had favoured him with her affections, and was determined to make her his wife. Since Vicky was equally determined, there was little for Marissa to do but make the best of the situation.

It did not get any easier. As Mrs Beaumont, Vicky ran Grafton Court entirely to suit herself, and that meant spending money whenever she felt the need, which was fairly often. It was not unnatural for a new wife to want to make some changes, but Marissa could not help resenting it when treasured pieces of family furniture disappeared, to be replaced by something garishly modern and out of keeping with the character of the house. When her own bedroom was completely redecorated and refurbished without her being consulted, she had her first open, full-blown argument with her stepmother.

Trembling with rage and distress, she hurled cushions on the floor and swept ornaments off the hated new dressing-table, while Vicky stood blinking in apparently wounded innocence, and her father hovered impotently in the background.

'But, Marissa . . . darling . . . I thought *all* girls your age adored pink . . . these curtains are so pretty, and it was high time you had some new furniture to replace all that hideous, old-fashioned stuff!'

'I hate pink! I liked my furniture—I liked my room the way it was!' Marissa declared mutinously. 'And where are all my horse prints? I hate all these sweet little icky dancing cherubs! You did it all without even asking me! How *could* you?'

'*Cariad*, I think Vicky wanted it to be a surprise for you,' her father interrupted soothingly, and, beyond the stage where she could be calmed, Marissa whirled on him too.

'Don't call me that! Don't ever call me that again!' '*Cariad*' had been her Welsh mother's endearment. Marissa could hardly remember her, beyond a persistent image of dark hair and a haunting softness, but she knew that reflective, gentle woman would not have ridden roughshod over a teenager's passionate, confused feelings.

Only when they were alone, Vicky's injured sensitivities disappeared instantly, and she regarded the still angry girl with a hard, speculative stare.

'I am your father's wife, Marissa, whether you like it or not—this is my house, and I'll have things here the way I want them. You'll have to accept that.

And it's no use appealing to your father over my head, because if it comes to a contest between us, I'll win,' she said, quietly but with evident triumph. 'He'll do anything I ask, and I have weapons you have no notion of. Never forget that.'

From that moment Marissa was on the downhill slide. The atmosphere at Grafton Court was far from harmonious, but Vicky cleverly managed to make it appear that this was all Marissa's fault. Her father, she knew, thought she was simply being difficult, a classic reaction of jealousy towards an unwanted step-parent. But Marissa would have been perfectly amenable to his remarriage to any of half a dozen eligible women who had visited Grafton Court over the years, most of them local ladies with country backgrounds and an understanding of growing daughters. Only he had had to choose Vicky, who disliked the country and ignored it as far as possible, who wanted to turn Grafton Court into a Sunday-supplement town house, and who, since she could not cancel out Marissa's existence, would settle for making her life a misery.

She endured it for almost a year, and on her eighteenth birthday decided that enough was enough. Since Vicky was here to stay, and there was no way they could co-exist happily, it followed that she must be the one to leave. In a sense, she knew, it was admitting defeat, but she told herself that there were times when retreat was the only possible strategy.

She told her father only that she considered it was time for her to move out into the world and create a life of her own. There was no point in heaping up recriminations, which he would most likely dismiss. He was married to Vicky, and so completely under her thumb that he could not bear any criticism of her.

'But where will you go—what will you do?' he asked, sincerely puzzled. 'I always thought you loved it here.'

'I do.' Marissa shrugged, trying not to think about how much it was going to hurt her to leave. 'But I want to get a job, and jobs are mostly in cities. I expect I'll be back from time to time,' she added lightly, as much to cheer herself up as to console him.

For it wouldn't be the same, she knew. To come home as a visitor was not to be compared with living here, watching the slow turn of the seasons, the red soil springing to life every year, the summers drowsy with bees and blossom and the scent of cider apples, the scarlet coats of the hunt outside the local inn every autumn, horses' hooves clattering impatiently in the yard, the quiet blanket of snow cradling the winter hills in a comforting embrace. During those last weeks before her departure, she thought her heart was being slowly drawn from her body, bit by bit. She counted the days away, like one facing exile; nearer, nearer it drew, it was unbearable, but she could do nothing to prevent what had to be. And when at last the day came, she felt like Adam and Eve in Milton's Paradise Lost.

"They hand in hand, with wandering steps and slow
From Eden took their solitary way . . . "

Except that they, at least, had one another, and she was quite alone.

She stayed with an old schoolfriend in London

while she determinedly did the rounds of job-hunting, gradually becoming more and more dispirited as she realised she was not exactly qualified for anything. Yes, she'd had a reasonably good education, but could she type? No, she couldn't. Use computers? Not really. Everything, it seemed, required further training, and her aim was to be self-sufficient, immediately. She could not go crawling home explaining that she needed support for a further two or three years' college course.

The only thing she could find there and then was a waitress's job in a cafe, and she had to admit that she was not very good at it. Nor would it pay enough to keep her once she left her friend's hospitality behind her. They were in no way eager to be rid of her, but Marissa was fiercely anxious to be independent and a burden to no one, and so far failed to see how she might accomplish this ambition.

Coming home one evening, her feet aching, wrung out mentally and physically, and with the exasperated complaints of the cafe's proprietor still ringing in her ears, she dropped exhaustedly into a chair in the lounge. Suzanne, her friend, had a visitor, a young man, she noted, wishing it was not so, because she really did not have enough energy left to be sociable. As soon as she could summon up the effort required, she would go to her room, she decided.

But the young man was looking at her in a most peculiar way—appraisingly, although not, she thought, sexually, like the café customers who sometimes tried to put their arms covertly around her, or eyed her lecherously while she took their orders.

'Hey, Sue!' he said reproachfully. 'How come you never told me your friend was such a stunner?'

Marissa paled, afraid that if he were one of Suzanne's boyfriends she would not take too kindly to this. But he turned out to be her cousin, and a professional photographer.

'Have you ever considered modelling?' he asked, two cups of coffee later, after she had revived a little, and they'd all laughed over her summary of a disastrous day at the café. 'I reckon you'd be ideal—how tall are you? Five-eight? Nine? Stand up...no, I'm serious...turn around...slowly...'

'This is silly!' Marissa protested as she pivoted self-consciously for his inspection. But within minutes she was turning her head, her body, moving and posing at his direction until he declared delightedly that she was a 'natural'.

'You'll need a portfolio of photos, of course, but I'd be glad to take some shots of you,' he said. Marissa shrugged and agreed—she still wasn't taking this seriously, but she had nothing to lose. Only when she saw the photos did she realise the immensity of her own potential, a glorious natural asset she had lived all her life unaware of. The camera, quite simply, loved her, and in less than a week a model agency had put her on its books.

It had not been instant, overnight success. Young and uncertain, she had had to learn her craft, and at first she had kept on her job at the café. But Marissa had the kind of beauty that did not depend on extreme youth, and as she matured it bloomed and improved. By the time she was twenty she was heavily in demand, and hers was the haunting face that smiled wistfully from glossy magazine covers, hers the long-limbed elegance enhancing top fashion articles.

Her work took her all over the world now, and she was based in London where she shared a flat with another girl. From time to time, as she had promised, she did return home to Herefordshire, but her visits were usually short. Now that she was a grown woman, with a flourishing career of her own, she was no longer intimidated by Vicky, and most of the time a guarded truce was maintained between them, marred by a little occasional sniping. Vicky, she guessed shrewdly, was a little resentful of her success, but at least now she could not tease her about long-legged gawkiness, when her looks and her style were acclaimed all over Europe and America.

Now, lying in bed, Marissa pieced together the events of the afternoon, her walk, and the encounter with the American who had told her he wanted to buy Grafton Court. She recalled his complex, interesting face, his large but limber body...what was he? What sort of a man would want to buy a run-down mediaeval manor house with so much land? He had not looked like the archetypal country squire to her. And yet...

Oh, what did it matter? Why should she even be puzzling her mind about him, his motives, or his background, when the whole point at issue was her father's intention to sell? To whom was not important...was it?

She opened her eyes carefully, finding the light painful, and saw Dr Pritchard standing by her bedside. He'd been their family doctor since Marissa was a child, and his father before him; indeed, as he often joked, the practice seemed to run in his family.

She smiled wanly, and he returned the smile, taking her wrist and finding the pulse.

'Hello, young woman. Heard you were convalescing, and I was intending to drop by and see you, but I hadn't expected to be summoned here already,' he said.

'Sorry, Dr Pritchard. I expect I was overdoing things,' she croaked. 'I haven't done much walking lately, and hadn't realised I'd exerted so much effort.'

She frowned. Who had found her and brought her in? she wondered. One of her father's estate workers, she supposed—she truly could not remember anything that had happened between talking to the American and waking up here.

'Yes, indeed,' he said sternly. 'Exercise is fine, Marissa, in moderation, but build it up slowly, a little at a time. And rest—you still need lots of it. You've been seriously ill, and shouldn't forget it.'

'All right, doctor,' she agreed meekly. Right now she was in no state to argue with anyone, and she could see the wisdom of his advice. 'I promise to take things gradually, although I won't be a prisoner in the house.'

'No one who knows you expects that, Marissa,' he said with a grin. 'You were always an outdoor girl—can't think how you stand all those studios and lights. Just remember what I told you, and don't give me any hassle! I'm only keeping this practice warm until my Ruth can take over—then you'll never see me without a fishing rod!'

They chatted briefly about his daughter's work at a large city hospital, then he said, 'I'd better go and reassure your father that you're suffering nothing worse than exhaustion—unless you've had some kind of shock you aren't telling me about?'

His oblique query was left unanswered and, alone, Marissa wondered if *he* knew about her father selling Grafton Court, and if he did, what he thought. Beaumonts had lived here for so long that she was sure most of the local people would see their moving out as the breaking of an invisible but tenuous bond of trust. The old order changes . . . but does it have to be destroyed entirely? she mused wearily.

When her bedroom door opened it was Vicky who came in, not her father. Marissa eyed her dispassionately. She wore a dusky pink velour jogging suit—not that she ever did anything more energetic than trot round the department stores—and round her neck were several fine-meshed gold chains, inset with tiny red stones, which had been the cause of the argument they'd had before Marissa lit out. The stones were rubies, not even garnets, and yet Grafton Court needed re-roofing in several places—damp seeped in the dining-room whenever it rained—boundary fences required replacing in great lengths, and tenant farmers were anxious about lots of little jobs which were their landlord's—her father's—responsibility.

'If my husband chooses to give me a present, that's his business, and mine—certainly not yours!' Vicky had flashed at her. 'You're just jealous because I mean more to him than you, and this mouldering old pile of plasterwork!'

Now she approached the bed somewhat cautiously, as she might the lair of a wild animal who could be expected to pounce.

'You gave us a bit of a scare,' she said lightly,

'but Dr Pritchard says you're going to be all right.'

Marissa did not for one moment think it was undue concern for her health which had sent Vicky up here, although that was probably the tale she had spun her husband, so she disregarded this overture.

'I *know*' she said. 'You don't have to bust a gut keeping quiet about it any longer. I know about Father wanting to sell Grafton Court.'

Her voice was quietly accusing, and Vicky bristled defensively.

'We should have told you straight away—I wanted to,' she said.

'I'll bet you did. And I imagine you're overjoyed.' Marissa could not keep the edge of sarcasm out of her voice.

'I'm not losing any sleep over it, that's for sure,' Vicky retorted tartly. 'It'll be a relief to get shot of this millstone and live life like any normal married couple, in a nice new house, with civilised amenities nearby. Anyhow, it's what your father wants, and that's what counts,' she added piously.

Marissa's laugh was ragged.

'Oh, sure! How long did it take you to persuade him?' she asked.

Vicky bridled.

'I don't have to put up with all this from you,' she declared. 'We're selling, and that's the end of it. I suppose *he* told you,' she finished significantly.

Marissa frowned. 'Who?' she asked, sounding stupid, even to her own ears.

Vicky clucked impatiently.

'The American, Rick Jablonski, of course. Who else?' she demanded.

Marissa was struggling back through the blank spaces in her memory. There was something . . . but she couldn't bring it clearly into focus.

'Jablonski?' She tasted the unfamiliar, foreign-sounding name. 'Is that what he's called? But how did you know I'd spoken to him?'

Vicky's harsh laughter came oddly from so small and delicate-seeming a creature.

'Don't you remember? You *have* to. It was he who brought you home! Carried you into the house as if you were something he'd shot,—said you'd fainted. *Very* dramatic, Marissa! But it won't work. Faint all you like—Grafton Court is still being sold. And that nice rich Mr Jablonski is going to turn it into a leisure park. What do you think of that?'

CHAPTER TWO

MARISSA was up and about again the day after her mishap, and wasted no time in confronting her father.

'I didn't want to tell you until you'd regained some of your strength,' he said, a little shamefaced.'I knew you'd be upset. It was just bad luck, your running into Jablonski like that.'

She grimaced.

'That terrible man—who is he? How can you think of selling to someone like that? Vicky says he's going to build a leisure park! Father, you can't let that happen to Grafton Court!'

'That terrible man, as you call him, took the trouble to bring you home yesterday—otherwise you might have been lying there unconscious for quite some time,' he reminded her. 'And Marissa, what he does with Grafton Court after he's bought it is, unfortunately, none of our business.'

'It's true, then?' she persisted.

'It's true that he owns a chain of leisure parks all over the US, and is keen to branch out into Europe,' he admitted. 'He's an ambitious young man, with lots of drive, and he can well afford what I'm asking. In fact, his offer is more than generous. Buyers like that don't fall out of the trees, you know.'

Marissa twisted her hands together, got up, and paced nervously up and down the room.

'Father, think again, that's all I'm asking. Grafton Court has been in our family for almost four hundred years. You can't just throw it away! We can manage to keep it if we all tighten our bets a little. I'll try and send more money——'

'You've already poured enough of what you earn into this white elephant, Marissa,' he said stubbornly. 'You're young, and you should be spending your money on yourself, enjoying life. I want to enjoy life a little too—take Vicky places, buy her things.'

'Vicky!' Marissa said bitterly. 'She's at the bottom of all this, I suppose!'

Her father looked so wretched that she felt sorry for him, even knowing him for what he was, a charming but weak-willed man.

'Don't blame her too much, Marissa,' he begged. 'She's young too, and doesn't want to spend all her life isolated here, denying herself life's luxuries on account of an uneconomical old house that eats up money.'

Marissa had not seen much evidence of self-denial in the years since her father married Vicky. Suddenly, it had seemed, there had been money for things which had previously been lacking—clothes, jewellery, trips, new furniture. She wondered fleetingly how much her father was in debt, how much of the money she'd regularly contributed from her earnings to the upkeep of Grafton Court had been spent on providing those 'little luxuries'.

'She knew when she married you—every woman who marries a Beaumont knows that she's taking on Grafton Court. It's a trust,' she said implacably.

Her father was becoming impatient.

'We're not living in the Middle Ages now, Marissa,' he said testily. 'It's just a house. Only the very rich can afford to keep up these old places nowadays. And there won't be Beaumonts to inherit, since when you marry you'll no longer be one.'

That hurt, and she gazed at him reproachfully.

'Well, I'm sorry I turned out to be female!' she retorted. 'But you and Vicky could remedy that lack easily enough.'

'Vicky won't have children while we're living here. She's not happy—feels imprisoned,' he said shortly.

So that was the bribe, the carrot which was being dangled in front of him! Vicky, as she had intimated all those years ago, certainly had weapons Marissa could not match. She was bows and arrows to her stepmother's heavy artillery, she reflected miserably.

'There doesn't seem to be anything I can say or do to change your mind,' she said dully.

'There isn't. I *have* to sell, Marissa. I simply can't afford not to,' he insisted. 'I know you're upset now, but you have all your life in front of you. You'll get over it. One day you'll have a husband and a family, and a home of your own, and you'll be able to think of this house simply as a place where you grew up.'

Marissa was not won over by this facile argument. Grafton Court was not just a house, a 'place where she grew up'. It was a link in a living chain, stretching back across the centuries, a chain of which she felt herself to be a vital, breathing part. This land, its hills, fields and woods, were deeply ingrained in her, as she was in it, so that she could not say where it left off and she began. She did not understand why she was so strongly aware of this fierce symbiosis, and her father was not. Perhaps all chains had strong links and weaker ones, and his was the thinly extruded section which would finally snap. To give place to what? That wretched man Rick Jablonski, and his leisure park?

Nausea welled up in her, and she turned her back and stood staring out of the window at the lawns, surrounded by their bright beds of spring flowers, and the orchard beyond. Since she did not answer him, her father assumed he had won the argument, and brightened perceptibly.

'Good girl—I know it's been a shock, but once you've got used to the idea, I'm sure you'll see it's the only way,' he said cheerfully. 'Now why don't you go and get changed? I've invited Mr Jablonski to join us for drinks before lunch.'

Marissa turned, gazing at him in horrified disbelief.

'That man—coming here for drinks?' she repeated incredulously. 'That's like…well, it's like fraternising with the enemy!'

'He's not our enemy,' Davis Beaumont said irritably. 'Why won't you be sensible about this, Marissa? He's giving me a good price, and there's no reason why we shouldn't be amicable about it. Furthermore, he did you a good turn the other day and, whatever your personal opinion, you ought to have the good manners to thank him.'

'I wouldn't have needed his help if he hadn't given me the shock of my life in the first instance,' she said stubbornly.

And then, for the first time, she remembered it

all, exactly as it had happened. She saw herself running, breathless, Idris loping along at her side, felt the pain in her chest and in her head, as her strength failed her...then the panic of collapse, with the dog licking her face...and blackness.

He must have followed her, seeing that she was in no condition to run like that, traced her to the copse, and carried her home. He'd picked her up and carried her, as if she had been a baby...she remembered the size and breadth of him. It could not have been any great hardship to a man so built. And Idris must have let this strange man lay hands on her, knowing instinctively that he did not mean her any harm.

Marissa was swamped by strange, inexplicable emotions at the thought of all this happening to her while she knew nothing of it. Being held, touched...

'He carried you in as if you were something he'd shot,' she heard Vicky's amused, dismissive voice, and shook herself. It hadn't mattered to him that she was in trouble, only in so far as she was the daughter of the man with whom he was about to clinch a deal. It wouldn't have been politic to leave her lying in the wood! This realisation left her feeling oddly bereft, as if someone had just taken away a solid wall which was supporting her, and this annoyed her for the simple reason that she did not understand why it should be so.

All the same, her father did have a point.

'Oh, very well, I'll say thank you, if it will make everybody happy,' she said ungraciously. 'But I'm not going to get changed. Mr. Jablonski will just have to take me as I am.'

On this she was adamant. She was not going to dress up and go to a lot of trouble for the man who was going to turn her out of her home. She was wearing a pair of loose, beige twill trousers and a chocolate-brown, short-sleeved sweater with a knobbly texture. Her hair was brushed back from her face to fall as it chose around her slight shoulders, and her only adornment was a pair of cameo earrings which had been her mother's, and a matching ring. Her feet were slipped easily into a pair of espadrilles she had bought in Spain, and wore endlessly indoors because they were so comfortable.

Her casual apparel and un-made-up face were sure to give Rick Jablonski the message she wanted to put across. I'm going to thank you, because I've been properly brought up, and know I have to, but I'm damned if I'll tart myself up for your delectation, because I don't like you, or anything you stand for—that message shouted out, loud and clear.

She almost faltered in her purpose when Vicky slunk down, nattily turned out in an expensive little crêpe de Chine suit, her hair fluffed out artfully around her appealing face, pearl and diamanté drops swinging from her dainty ears. But Marissa straightened her shoulders resolutely. The contrast between the two of them should drive the message home even more firmly—unless Mr Rick Jablonski were so dense and unperceptive that he could not take a hint if it were not posted up in six-foot-high neon lights. Should one expect too much sensitivity from a man who built leisure parks? she wondered.

The nagging little voice of her own conscience told her she was being unfair. He had not seemed to lack perception, picking up at once the fragility she tried so hard to hide. But he was still the man who was going to buy Grafton Court. She could not allow herself the weakness of admiring anything about him.

Vicky glanced at her with disdainful amusement.

'We're expecting a visitor, dear, didn't you know? You look more as if you're about to go out and dead-head the daffodils,' she said sweetly.

Marissa looked down at her, quite deliberately. These days her height did not embarrass her.

'That's exactly what I had in mind,' she replied, with equal saccharine sweetness. 'I can't see the necessity for being overdressed.'

She sat down, crossing one knee elegantly over the other, aware that there was something about her length of leg that always enraged Vicky, who was short in that department. These were all meagre triumphs, petty victories, she knew, in her own heart. They did nothing to compensate for the fact that the battle went to Vicky, and gave her hurt spirits no more than a momentary ease.

Rick Jablonski arrived promptly at twelve-thirty, shook hands politely with Davis and Vicky, then turned to Marissa with a little enquiring smile just touching the mobile corners of his lips.

'Miss Beaumont? I hope you're feeling better today?'

Marissa allowed him to take her hand. His fingers were warm and dry, their grip light but strong. Hands that could crush you, she thought, or touch a butterfly without harming it—as he chose. The image surprised her, and she drew her hand away a little too quickly.

'I'm fine, Mr. Jablonski, and I must thank you for coming to my aid yesterday,' she said, with cool courtesy.

'There's no "must" about it. Thank me if you so wish, but you're under no obligation to do so,' he replied levelly, picking up on that one word as if he knew that her gratitude was a trifle forced.

Marissa stared at him, slightly affronted, and not a little surprised. He didn't play by the rules. He was supposed to get her message, but not to respond overtly to it, and she had to conclude that he felt no compunction about embarrassing her.

'That wasn't what I meant,' she said quickly, in some confusion.

'Wasn't it?' The strong eyebrows rose, creating again that intriguing furrow across the brow. Marissa found herself watching it with an unholy fascination she did not understand, unaware that an awkward little silence had fallen.

'Marissa's a little upset about the sale of the house,' said Vicky, with a sympathy which sounded sincere enough to fool anyone. 'She was born here, you know, and it's hit her hard.'

'I do understand,' Rick Jablonski said, but although he was answering her stepmother his blue-green eyes did not leave Marissa's face—much to Vicky's chagrin, she saw. Vicky liked male attention of any kind to be focused exclusively on herself. Well, she was welcome to this man's! Not even for the undoubted pleasure of annoying Vicky did Marissa want to remain in the spotlight of that oddly discerning gaze which seemed to look right through into the unpleasant secrets of her troubled mind.

'Where is your home, Mr Jablonski?' she enquired, with a coolness meant to imply that she was not really interested, just making polite conversation.

'Rick, please. In the States, surnames seldom persist after the introduction.' He paused, considering her question. 'I'm not really sure how to answer that one. I was born in New York, but my family moved around a lot. Then I went to California as a young man, and spent some years out there. Now I expect to be in Europe for quite some time. I guess you might call me a professional vagrant!'

A pirate, more like, Marissa thought distastefully—roaming around, seizing on acres of unspoiled land and building hideous excrescences on them! She accepted the vermouth her father automatically poured for her, Vicky had her usual sweet sherry, and Rick Jablonski asked for vodka.

Davis poured generously.

'What would you like in it—lime, tonic?'

'Just as it comes. A little ice.' Rick drank half the fiery liquid without a tremor, and smiled slightly at his companions' surprise. 'My parents, as you might guess from my name, were Polish. They went to America after the war, when the map of Europe was so re-drawn that they had nowhere on it to call theirs. My father kept the language and customs all his life. If I were to keep up with him, I really should down the lot in one swallow!'

'And smash the glass into the fireplace, no doubt,' Marissa said drily.

The smile lingered on her, pleasant, unaltered, so why did she feel threatened by it? Was it the icy glitter in his eyes which warned her he was not a man to try making a fool of?

'Oh, no, Marissa. These are best Bohemian lead crystal, and it would be sacrilege,' he said lightly.

She shrugged.

'And they'll be yours soon, so it would be a shame to break them' she persisted tauntingly, knowing it was cowardly of her, really, not daring, for she suspected cravenly that had they been alone in the room, she would not have pushed him so far. She saw his knuckles whiten as his fingers tightened around the stem of the glass, and the smiling mouth narrow into a thin, cold line. *One day, those glittering eyes promised her, I'll make you very sorry for those words!*

'I'm sure Mrs Beaumont will be wanting these in her new home,' he said hurtfully. 'All I require is the land—Marissa.'

She looked at him with huge, wounded, tawny-dark eyes, both hating and fascinated by the way he spoke her name, lengthening the middle syllable to give it a faint Eastern European intonation. *I'm going to bring in bulldozers and raze this place to the ground until there's nothing left of the ancient half-timbering but a square patch of raw earth*, that narrow-lipped smile told her with satisfaction. She shivered, feeling as exposed and helpless as if he had threatened to violate her, and there was nothing she could do to stop him having his desecrating way.

Davis hurried anxiously to refill the glasses.

'You're being rather rude and provocative, Marissa,' he said curtly. 'You must forgive my daughter...er...Rick. As my wife explained, she's not too happy about the sale, although I've tried to make her understand my reasons. And she hasn't been well.'

'So I guessed. Some bug you picked up abroad, was it?' He looked almost solicitous, but Marissa did not allow herself to be fooled.

'In Africa. But really my father exaggerates. I'm quite well,' she lied shortly, anxious not to appear to be demanding his sympathy.

He looked at her consideringly.

'Do you travel a lot? I ask because I seem to know you, somehow. You're an actress, perhaps? No? I'm sure I've seen your face some place before.'

She smiled thinly.

'Not unless you read fashion magazines, Mr Jablonski. Or perhaps your wife does.'

It wasn't curiosity, she insisted. She really didn't care, one way or the other, but he would appear to be in his mid-thirties, and most men of that age had wives and families. But his smile was knowing—I'll tell you what it is you're itching to find out, it said.

'I'm not married. But I have friends, and *they* read fashion magazines, so perhaps that's the answer. You're a model?'

She inclined her head in acknowledgement, but before any discussion of Marissa's career was embarked on Vicky jumped in, deciding that her stepdaughter had monopolised the visitor for too long, and proceeded to bombard him with questions about New York and California. She'd never been to America, she told him, but it must be fascinating. So new, so vast, so exciting, etc, etc....well, who knew, perhaps they'd make a trip over, this year...this with an oblique, triumphant little glance at Marissa, while her father's attention was elsewhere.

Rick answered all her questions patiently and politely, but he did not appear bowled over by her limpid blue gaze and come-hither eyelashes, Marissa observed. So Vicky wasn't his type? What kind of woman did he admire, then? Who the hell cares? she thought angrily, draining her glass in a gulp.

He refused another drink with a shake of the head.

'I have to drive, unfortunately.'

'Oh, but you *must* stay to lunch,' Vicky insisted, her hand on his arm.

'I can't, I'm afraid, Mrs Beaumont...Vicky...as I told your husband when he phoned, I have a previous appointment,' he said. 'But thank you for your hospitality. It goes to prove that the British are not really as stand-offish as we're led to believe.' Did his eyes flicker very slightly in Marissa's direction? 'Well, most of them aren't.'

She uncoiled herself from her chair, and to her father's evident surprise said, 'I'll show Mr Jablonski out, Father. You and Vicky go in to lunch.'

He smiled affably, relieved that she seemed to want to redeem herself and make amends for her lack of courtesy. But he was easy to deceive, believing mostly what he wished to believe, Marissa thought, as she walked out into the bright spring day at Rick Jablonski's side. Not like *this* man...

'Was there something you wanted to say to me privately, Marissa?' he asked, the smile disarmingly gentle now, but totally undeceived.

'Just this.' She turned and looked back at Grafton Court, its white plasterwork mellow against the black timbers, its old walls nowhere completely straight, but everywhere leaning endearingly at an angle. 'I love this house. You probably won't understand how much, since, as you say, you've moved around a lot. But my family has lived here since Tudor times, if English history means anything to you. Before I'll let you come in here with your JCBs and pull it down, I'll put a torch to it!'

He let his leonine head fall back, and laughed out loud with genuine appreciation. As quickly, then, his laughter ceased, and placing one of his large, strong hands on each of her shoulders, he looked down into her eyes with cold, stern intentness.

'I may admire your guts, Marissa, but what you're threatening to do is arson, and you'll find yourself spending several years at Her Majesty's residential hotel at Holloway if you attempt anything so foolish,' he said incisively. 'And don't ever doubt that I'd help to put you there, my little firebrand. *Dzen dobre…*or should I say, have a nice day.'

Marissa stood rooted to the spot, watching as he climbed into a flamboyantly elegant sports car and drove away. What left her speechless—breathless, almost— was not his derisive laughter, or the threat she didn't hesitate to believe he would carry out. It was the strange, not entirely unpleasant sensation of being referred to—she, Marissa Beaumont, five nine and a half in her stockinged feet—as 'my *little* firebrand.'

Grafton Court stood just outside the small village of Bishopswell, and Marissa rode in next morning, leaving her chestnut mare, Salome, to graze in the field at the rear of the Black Lion Hotel.

Bishopswell and the surrounding area had obviously, in the Middle Ages, supported a much larger population than it did now, as could be evinced from the size of the church, its tall spire a visible landmark for many miles around. Marissa gazed across the bowling green to the churchyard, noting the furled buds of the magnolia tree by the porch, which would be in full, creamy flower in a week or two, given good weather.

Turning, she walked up the main street, which still contained a high proportion of black and white fourteenth and fifteenth-century houses, greeting people she knew...which was just about everyone in the village. Any face she did not know would belong to a stranger, most probably a tourist admiring the old buildings nestling in their serene backdrop of green, wooded hills.

Her father and Vicky had given her letters to post—the latter's addressed to a high-class mail order company, she noted dourly—and she had several of her own, so her trip involved a wait at the Post Office counter. The Post Office, its walls painted white, windows spilling over with flower-filled boxes, was tiny, and more than three people inside it constituted a queue. A good amount of local gossip was disseminated here, and Mrs Jones and Mrs Price, just in front of her, returned eagerly to theirs after greeting Marissa. Ahead of them, old Mr Williams was filling in a form with the assistance of Sylvia behind the counter, and Marissa knew from long experience that this would necessitate a considerable wait.

But no one seemed to mind, or to be in a hurry. There was all day, and failing that, tomorrow, friends to chat to while one waited, and the prospect of meeting others outside in the street, or in the general store. Unknown to herself, a smile curved her mouth. It was all so different from London, where people scarcely had time to wish one good morning, and from the hustle and confusion of airports and hotels which were a large part of her working life.

'Holy smoke!' a familiar voice said softly behind her. 'I only dropped by for an airmail letter! How long will it take, do you reckon?'

The smile froze on Marissa's lips as she turned her head. Rick Jablonski's large frame seemed to fill the doorway of the tiny building, and he had to stoop to enter at all. She felt trapped and enveloped by his presence—both physically and mentally, he demanded and appropriated a lot of space.

'You might be out by a week next Tuesday, with a bit of luck,' she replied airily, trying to convince herself that she was not troubled by him. 'No one rushes here—there's no need to. Not much has changed in a hundred years—nor would it, if people left it alone,' she added, with some acidity.

'You don't like change?' he asked, unworried by her side-swipe of a hint.

'Not for its own sake. Only if it can guarantee something better,' she replied shortly.

'Hm,' he said thoughtfully. 'Unfortunately, life doesn't come with money-back-if-not-satisfied guarantees. You have to take chances, make mistakes, discard what doesn't work along the way. I guess that's called evolution.'

Marissa surveyed him with a jaundiced eye.

'You imagine you're pretty smart, don't you?' she challenged. 'But it will take more than you think to change rural Herefordshire, or its people. They're bedded into the soil with a slow, stubborn, resistant quality, and will give you short shrift if they don't like what you're doing.'

'What makes you so sure I *want* to change it?' he demanded lightly. 'You're hot at jumping to conclusions. Do you ever stop to think before you leap?'

She gave a short, hard laugh.

'Oh, really! It would be naïve to contend that a thumping great leisure park slapped down in the countryside isn't going to affect its character. You've seen the roads, how narrow they are—how are all your coaches going to get in? Easy—you widen the lanes, cut down the hedges. And then the car parks—just plough up a few farms...' She choked a little, the emotion she had promised herself not to give way to overcoming her, despite her best efforts, and the fatigue she was still fighting to conquer flooding back.

Mr Williams, his form completed, ambled out of the Post Office, Rick almost pinning himself to the wall to give him room to pass, and the two ladies took his place. They too seemed to have a good deal of business to attend to. Marissa foresaw another five or ten minutes cramped up against this powerful, detestable man, with whom she was sure to argue and upset herself further.

'Look,' she said, 'if you've something else to do, I'll get your airmail letter for you. I'll be here for some time.'

'Good idea,' he said, reaching into his pocket and fishing out a handful of coins. 'This ought to cover it, right? Meet me in the bar of the Black Lion when you've done.'

And then he was gone, without giving her time to protest. Marissa clamped her lips tightly together to suppress her gasp of outrage. What she had wanted was to get rid of him, her idea being that he could come back in a few minutes for his letter. She hadn't planned on any kind of rendezvous with him.

When her turn came, Marissa bought her stamps and his airmail letter, and posted her mail. She then called in the general store for one or two items she wanted, and at the newspaper shop. In both of these she was inevitably involved in conversations, questions about her health and how long she would be staying, enquiries about the 'Squire' as many of the older people still referred to her father. A good twenty minutes had passed before she made her way back down the street towards the Black Lion, she observed, with a guilty glance at the church clock.

Well, so what? It had been his idea for her to meet him there—if he'd called back at the Post Office he could have had his wretched letter sooner, she thought irritably, and there was no need for her to run like a truant schoolgirl late for assembly! Deliberately she slowed her pace and strolled the rest of the way. Running still left her breathless, and she most definitely did not want him thinking she'd hurried on his account!

The Black Lion was an old coaching inn, the low beams in its lounge bar were the genuine article, not a facet of the restorer's art. The oak settles and tables were old too, there were bundles of dried hops hung above the bar, and a vast fireplace, big enough to roast an ox, but now filled with an artistic decoration composed of spring flowers.

Rick was leaning on the bar, chatting to Gillian Cooke, the landlord's wife.

'Here you are at last,' he said as she entered. 'You took so long, the ice has melted in your Martini.'

'I told you, no one hurries here,' she replied smartly. 'And I don't recall asking for a drink, anyhow. Slip it in your vodka.'

'Not a chance.' He pushed the glass in front of her. '*I* told *you*, nothing goes in my vodka. Shall we go and sit down?'

The drink, it seemed, she had to have, but she was not going to make herself comfortable and turn it into a session. Marissa perched on the edge of a bar stool.

'I'm fine right here,' she insisted.

'OK' Rick signalled for another drink for himself. 'Put these on my account, please, Mrs Cooke.'

Marissa glanced at him in surprise.

'I didn't know you were staying here.'

'Probably because you didn't ask,' he observed easily. His eyes lazily traversed the length of her, from the top of her dark head, hair neatly pinned in a chignon beneath her hard riding hat to the toe of her brown leather boots. 'Do you wear jodhpurs because you look good in them, or is the horse tethered to the saloon door, Annie Oakley?'

Marissa tried, and failed, to repress a grin. An awful suspicion was dawning on her that she might have found Rick Jablonski entertaining, if he had not been precisely who he was.

'No, she's grazing in the field at the back,' she said. 'I always leave her there when I come into Bishopswell. Gillian's daughter Laura grooms and exercises her for me while I'm away, so Salome is as much hers as mine.'

'Mm. I somehow can't imagine your stepmother undertaking that task,' murmured Rick, still with laughter in his voice. 'I'd say she's a drawing-room, not an outdoors woman.'

'Vicky, on horseback? Don't make me

laugh!'Marissa could not keep the edge of scorn from her voice, and Rick said,

'It doesn't take an expert on human relations to work out that you two don't get on like a house on fire. She's…not exactly averse to the sale of Grafton Court.'

It was really nothing at all to do with him how matters stood at home, and it was on the tip of Marissa's tongue to tell him to mind his own damn business. Surprisingly, then, she heard herself saying, 'If it weren't for Vicky, you wouldn't have any sale.'

'Marissa, don't fool yourself. Your father is in dire financial straits,' Rick said quietly. 'If he sells, he can live comfortably, investing some of what he realises. If he struggles on, he'll dig himself deeper into the mire. Believe me, I know what I'm talking about.'

'He wouldn't have *been* in dire financial straits if he hadn't married Vicky, if *I'd* taken over the running of Grafton Court,' she replied curtly. 'We'd never have been rich, but there would have been no extravagance, and we'd have broken even.'

'Maybe, but look, you wouldn't have had fame and success and an international career, would you?' he asked, and she looked up at him, the tawny eyes huge with pain.

'Do you think it compensates?'

'I don't know.' His reply was direct, with an undoubted ring of honesty. 'We have to take what life hands out, and re-shape it as best we can. We have to wrest our own destinies, often from unpromising material.'

'Is that what you did?' The question was involuntary, out before she could reconsider it.

'In a way. My people arrived in America very young, with nothing, and my father... well, he tried, but none of his schemes made his fortune, so I started out with nothing. What I have grew from small beginnings.'

For the last few minutes, Marissa realised, astonished, she had been talking to him almost as if he were sympathetic to her, on her side. She had to remind herself that the reverse was true.

'Oh, great! Terrific!' she cried. 'So in order to continue re-shaping the grand destiny of Rick Jablonski, you have to tear down a piece of living history, despoil great tracts of lovely countryside, and ruin my life into the bargain!'

'I don't think so, Marissa,' he said calmly, never moving his tall bulk, his eyes unflinching as she hurled this tirade at him.

'You don't think so!' she echoed fiercely. 'Then you must be out of your head! What else do you think your wretched leisure park is going to do?' She slammed her glass down on the bar, turned and rushed out, leaving Gillian Cooke and a handful of her regulars gazing after her in puzzled amazement.

Rick found her in the field round the back, leaning her head against the horse's soft muzzle. She wouldn't look at him, but, not sufficiently under control to ride, stood still, her back defiantly turned.

'This is definitely the last time I chase after you when you throw one of your stunts, lady,' he said sternly.

'Did I ask you to?' she demanded.

'No, but you have a disturbing habit of passing out,' he reminded her. 'Aren't you under doctor's orders to take it easy?'

'That's none of your business.'

'The hell it isn't! When a woman's in my company, I get this odd sensation of being responsible for her,' he declared. 'I dare say it's not very modern of me. Maybe it's a throwback to some old Polish habit, but there it is.'

Just for a moment, ever so briefly and fleetingly, a thought flickered through Marissa's weary mind. She thought that perhaps a woman who had Rick Jablonski responsible for her would never need be afraid of anything else. But she was not such a woman, for he and she were destined to be on opposite sides of the fence.

Slowly, unwillingly, she turned to face him, to find his big hand stroking Salome's gentle nose. A city-bred man, who had spent all his life struggling to the top...by his own admission, the son of penniless immigrants...what would he know about horses? But the mare whickered softly and blew in his ear, and he seemed quite at ease with her.

'So this is Salome—quite a seductress. Living up to her name,' he said.

'I don't know about that. Once, maybe, but she's practically a pensioner now. I've had her since I was twelve,' Marissa replied. And then another thought struck her, which, astoundingly, she had not considered up to now. 'Oh lord, what will happen to the horses? Perhaps Laura... but this field isn't really big enough... she muttered, half to herself.

Rick put both hands on her shoulders, as he had the day before, but this time he gave her a slight but definite shake.

'Why don't you get the facts straight before you belt off at a tangent with all this doom-laden nonsense?' His voice was calm, but there was an edge of anger to it. 'You have me cast as this great ogre who's going to tear down your home and slap up a concrete complex in the middle of nowhere, but not once have you stopped to ask yourself, let alone ask *me* what I intended. Use your brain, Marissa, or I shall start believing the myth that all models are bimbos with cotton-wool between their ears!'

His finely controlled irritation stopped her in her tracks, leaving her devoid of speech, but her eyes were full of questions.

'I'm going to buy Grafton Court, that's true,' he said firmly. 'But I'm not going to turn it into a leisure park. That is not, nor ever was, a part of my plans!'

CHAPTER THREE

MORE than that he would not say, although Marissa was spilling over with questions.

'I'll talk to you some time when you've had chance to cool off and think.' he said, quite abruptly. 'I'm having lunch with my financial director, and, since he's come all the way from Los Angeles to Bishopswell so that I can thrash out some details, I don't intend wasting time I pay handsomely for.'

Since she could get no more out of him, Marissa mounted up and rode off in a huff. The only thing she could do was talk to her father, although she doubted that would help, since he had been under the same impression as she about Rick's future plans.

'To be honest, Marissa, I didn't press him too hard,' Davis Beaumont admitted, when she questioned him. 'No one else was likely to offer me anything like so good a price, and I didn't want to risk losing him.'

So you didn't even enquire what was to happen to a house which has been home to our family for four centuries, Marissa thought, a bitter distaste filling her mouth. But she said nothing. She and her father were never going to see eye to eye on this subject, and to argue further would only drive the wedge deeper between them.

Which would suit Vicky down to the ground, she

realised, noting the triumphant gleam in her stepmother's observant blue eyes.

'There will always be a place for you in our new home—you know that,' her father said, a trifle awkwardly.

'Dearest, Marissa will be far too busy to do more than flip through occasionally, once she's back modelling,' Vicky told him demurely. 'Especially when we aren't living at Grafton Court. But I expect we'll have a spare bedroom,' she added, making it sound for all the world as if she and her husband would be reduced to cramped circumstances.

Marissa got up and walked out of the room without troubling to reply. She and her father had never been especially close, but they had got along well enough, and it hurt her to see this chasm of disagreement widening between them. But there was very little she could do—Vicky held all the best cards.

She was left to wonder anew about Rick Jablonski's words. Had he been telling her the truth? Why should he lie to her, when he was perfectly at liberty to do what he chose with property *he* had purchased? She assumed he had gone through all the necessary planning applications before making a move, and unfortunately Grafton Court was not important enough to be a listed building.

He had been angry, she recalled, for all he had controlled it firmly, as if he were troubled by the assumptions she had made. But why should he care in the least what she thought—a man like that, who had bulldozed his way to riches and success? There was a riddle here which concerned Rick himself as much as his intentions. Although Marissa did not want to be personally intrigued by him, she could not resist this puzzle. Her mind kept returning to it again and again, and she knew she would have no peace until she got to the bottom of it.

It would have suited her ideally if she could have solved the mystery without having to meet him again.

There was no denying that he made her nervous. Lord knew, she had met plenty of men in the normal course of her life, photographers, journalists, advertising managers, but none of them was like Rick Jablonski. He was of a different breed, she wasn't altogether sure why. It might have something to do with the sheer size of him, which made her feel like a will-o'-the-wisp, insubstantial and easily snapped in two. But more likely, it was the abrasive, rough-edged personality, the inborn fighter's instinct that had enabled him to hack out a fortune from inauspicious beginnings. Unless you were born with a silver spoon in your mouth, you didn't get that far purely by being Mr Nice Guy, she reasoned. He must have stepped on a few necks, discarded a few scruples, wrecked a few careers along the way.

And yet he wasn't without compassion, nor, she thought, completely devoid of sensitivity. There was an inner mystery at the core of him, the sense of a natural, inbred quality which called to something similar in herself, making it impossible for her to dismiss him as simply a heartless machine for making money and wielding power...much as she would have liked to.

She dithered for the rest of the day, went to bed still undecided, and in the morning knew the minute she awoke that she could stand the uncertainty no longer. She had to know what he was planning, even if that meant speaking to him again.

She got out of bed, pulled on her dressing gown, and went downstairs. It was only eight o'clock, she could hear the housekeeper, Mrs Reed, moving about in the kitchen, but no one else was up. She could only hope that Rick was an early riser. He didn't strike her as the kind of man to lie abed when he could be up and about making deals that made money.

Very quietly she dialled the number of the Black Lion. There was only the one telephone extension at Grafton Court, situated in an alcove at the foot of the stairs, and she didn't want Vicky, particularly, listening in to her call.

It was Gillian Cooke herself who answered, sounding a little surprised when Marissa asked for Mr. Jablonski. Yes, he was still here—at least, she thought he was. He had had breakfast and paid his bill ten minutes ago, but she might just catch him in the car park. Marissa hung on, knowing that the mere fact of her calling him would be enough to start village gossips wagging their tongues, if Gill happened to mention it.

'Yes?' His voice was curt and businesslike, a man in a hurry. And now she did not know what to say.

'I...I wanted to talk to you...if it's convenient. It will only take a few minutes,' she stammered.

'It isn't. Not really,' he said incisively. 'Can you come to the point, Marissa? I was just about to leave, and I've got appointments in London this afternoon, and a plane to catch tonight.'

He was going back to the States? Marissa was trembly with panic. She would never know what was to hit her until it happened. No—she couldn't take that!

She thought of the telephone at the Black Lion, with Laura and the other Cooke children rushing past every few minutes, and the cleaner, Mandy Evans, who had the keenest ears in the village, interestedly polishing the brasses. With the dining-room door deliberately left wide open. And here—Vicky, for all she did not usually put in an appearance before ten, might well choose today to be perverse.

'I can't talk over the phone,' she said desperately. 'Please, Rick—just a few minutes.'

'So it's "please, Rick" now, is it?' he drawled with cutting amusement. 'You were a little less conciliatory last time we met, if I remember. Women can be so different when they want something.'

'I don't want anything from you—only information,' she snapped, feeling the tension in her rising to a pitch beyond her control. 'If that's asking too much, then forget it!'

'If you slam the phone down on me now, Marissa, this is the last you'll hear from me personally,' he said clearly, warningly. 'I have plenty of people working for me who can carry through my plans without my having to come near Grafton Court again. So listen. I'll be passing the bottom of your drive in ten minutes' time. I'll park and wait for precisely five minutes.'

Marissa gasped.

'But I'm not —'

A hint of cruel laughter was audible along the line.

'Not dressed?' he queried. 'Be there—in your

night shift, if necessary. I'll wait five minutes—no more.'

Hating him, Marissa sped upstairs to her bedroom. She had a quarter of an hour to wash, dress, make herself respectable and get to the bottom of the long, curving drive where the road passed the edge of the estate. Probably he thought no woman could do it, and probably a good many would fail in the attempt, but perhaps he had forgotten that she was a model and the quick-change was no stranger to her. She was in baggy black cords, a vast red and black checked overshirt, and neat black ankle boots in scarcely any time at all, her face clean, devoid of make-up, but lightly creamed with moisturiser, her hair whipped up into a jaunty flick of a ponytail.

And as he had promised, Rick was there at the bottom of the drive, in the red convertible with the soft top down, leaning comfortably on the wheel and flicking through the pages of a newspaper.

He pushed open the car door and she slipped into the passenger seat, trying to ignore the swift but thorough scrutiny of the aquamarine eyes.

'Good. Very few women can look so wholesome first thing in the morning, without their paint and powder,' he remarked. 'I approve, although I realise you're a professional.'

'I don't care for your approval,' she said coolly.

'You cared, twenty minutes ago, whether I agreed to see you or not,' he reminded her.

Marissa sighed.

'Yes, I was anxious to see you, but what I look like isn't important, nor is what you think of my appearance. Look, Mr Jablonski—Rick—I don't like you, or what you do, particularly. But you're buying my home from under me, and I'd like to know what you have in mind to do with it, if you're not, as you said, turning it into a leisure centre.'

He regarded her with cool speculation.

'A bird brain could work out that this area is not suitable for that,' he pointed out scathingly. 'You yourself mentioned the state of the access roads. There are no large centres of population near enough to mean anything—you British think anything over fifty miles is a long drive.'

He paused, continued to watch her with a perverse kind of enjoyment, as he might wind up a clockwork toy to see how it worked.

'So what do we have? We have a deeply rural area, absolutely stunning countryside, largely unspoiled, picturesque villages, old market towns, opportunities for riding, walking, fishing. In the middle of all this we have a rather nice old house, in need of plenty of attention, set in acres of beautiful grounds. I don't know what that suggests to you, Ms Firebrand Beaumont, but to my commercially inclined mentality it would seem to be the ideal set-up for a rather exclusive, up-market country-house hotel.'

Marissa did not even attempt to stifle the exclamation that escaped her.

'Grafton Court, a hotel!'

'One of those expensive places run more along the lines of a country club, for a very well-heeled and discriminating kind of customer,' he said, with a faint smile. 'Better than the hordes trampling all over your beloved acres, yeah? Since we must let in the public, let them pay well for the privilege. What's the matter?' She still looked stunned. 'I would have imagined that would appeal to your blue-blooded pretensions.'

Her chin shot up, and she glared at him with outright resentment.

'You're calling me a snob, and I object to that! I just want to...preserve what's here, what's been here for generations.'

'Then you should look on me as your saviour, not a twentieth-century version of Attila the Hun,' he observed mildly. 'I'm going to help achieve that end, Marissa. By selling to me, you'll be saving Grafton Court from some totally unappreciative speculator who'll demolish it and build a housing estate.'

His grin was almost wolfish, and there was no mistaking the mockery lurking in the depths of those level, no-nonsense tones. Marissa was too enraged for any response but a fierce, cleansing anger.

'If I'm a snob, Rick Jablonski, I don't know what that makes you!' she burst out. 'We were doing just fine here, without you and your kind! I don't need a second-generation Polish-American peasant to explain conservation to me!'

He caught both her wrists in one powerful hand, and imprisoned her, holding them so tightly she feared the bones would crack. His eyes were opaque and hard, his smile had disappeared into a thin, unpleasant line, and she felt it again... an emotion no man had ever aroused in her. Fear. Primitive and unreasoning, leaping along her veins and creating an unwilling excitement.

'I don't give a damn what you say about me personally, but leave my nationality and my antecedents well out of it!' he said harshly.

He reached across her with his free hand, as if to

open the car door and virtually push her out, then he seemed suddenly to change his mind. Instead, his hand closed around the base of her throat, thumb and index finger either side of her slim neck. She shivered, her eyes widened, but she was left to wonder, long afterwards, why she didn't struggle to get free. She didn't, even when his mouth imprisoned hers, hard and angry, biting her lips, forcing them open, not a seduction but an invasion. Right then, she didn't think at all, an impassioned exhilaration blotted out reason and sense until they were no longer part of her world. When he tore away from her, she was fighting for breath.

He did open the door, then.

'Right, out you get,' he ordered. 'And think yourself lucky that for me, business is business, and personal animosity has nothing to do with it.'

He left her standing at the side of the road, accelerated sharply and was gone in a cloud of blown dust. Marissa crossed her arms over her breasts, hugging herself as if for comfort and shuddering. It was just after eight-thirty, on, admittedly, a quiet country road, but public and in full daylight. Marissa dreaded to think what Rick might have done to her in a more private situation. She *did* think of it. That kiss had been almost an assault, but she had not protested. Not that her puny struggles could have prevented him from doing anything he really wanted, but would she have struggled if he had...oh, it didn't bear imagining! Marissa wiped her hand across her mouth, and instead of setting off back up the drive struck out for the open country, as if only punishing exercise could cleanse her of complicity in what had happened.

Breakfast was over when she arrived back at Grafton Court, and, feeling both tense and exhausted, she sought refuge in the Hall…as it had always been called, as it had originated as the Great Hall of mediaeval times, even though Vicky now referred to it as the 'lounge'. There she found a man in a pin-striped suit, walking around with a notebook and pen, scribbling busily.

She stared at him blankly, and he said, 'Good morning. I'm from the valuers' office.'

'I see,' was all she said, tonelessly, and turning abruptly, she traced her stepmother to the drawing-room where she was idly arranging flowers in a vase.

'There's a man in the Hall. He says he's from the valuers'.' Accusation hovered in her voice, even though she tried to remain calm.

'Then that's precisely who he is, dear,' Vicky said in a soft, placating but unmistakably jubilant tone. Her hands suddenly still, she said, 'Be reasonable, Marissa. Wherever your father and I decide to live, most modern houses aren't designed with rooms large enough for period furniture, so most of the old stuff that's left will have to go.'

'It didn't occur to you to ask *me* if I wanted any of it?' Marissa asked wretchedly.

'Darling. in that poky little shared flat of yours, where would you put it?' cooed Vicky, eyes wide.

'I won't always be living in a poky little shared flat—I earn good money,' Marissa pointed out. 'Perhaps I can afford something better, now I won't be shoring up your expensive tastes!'

Vicky's pert little crimsoned mouth fell open with outrage, for this was the first time Marissa had ever complained openly about the money she had poured into Grafton Court since her father's remarriage.

'Why, you …you insolent bitch!' she gasped, her hands clenched tightly.

'That's as may be, but I want that little French occasional table, and my mother's wing chair. Oh, and the piano,' Marissa retorted implacably. 'In fact, I'll make a list of my own, while the man from the valuers' is making his.'

Vicky's laughter was as shrill and indignant as a lemur's screech.

'Make as many lists as you like! You aren't getting any of it!' she vowed. 'That old stuff fetches good money nowadays, heaven only knows why, and your father and I need every penny of it! So keep your hands off!'

Marissa recalled Rick Jablonski saying seriously, 'Your father can live comfortably, investing some of what he realises,' and she was unmoved by this poverty-pleading. Somehow, unconsciously, she found herself echoing his speech patterns.

'The hell you do!' she said softly. 'I've pussyfooted around you for too many years, Vicky, trying to keep the peace, trying to find some way we could rub along. I left home because of you—not because I wanted to. And now you've run through as much money as you could lay hands on, you've persuaded my father he has no recourse other than to sell. Well, enough is enough! You're not having everything!'

By the time she reached her bedroom, her heart was pounding so violently in her chest, she thought it would explode. Locking the door firmly, she lay down on her bed and closed her eyes, but this time there was no merciful release of unconsciousness.

She was stronger now, and her brain would not obediently black out, sparing her more pain and anguish. She had to endure it, and she had to go on.

Marissa had never felt so alone and beleaguered. And once again, in this extremity of despair, she heard Rick's voice, firm and sure. ' We have to take what life hands out, and re-shape it as best we can.'

But how? 'Help me!' she whispered, and somehow it did not seem strange to her that she was appealing silently, across the miles that separated them, to the man who had treated her so roughly that very morning.

The matter of the furniture only illustrated Davis Beaumont's talent for prevarication. On the one hand, he would do almost anything to keep his wife sweet, and there was also a financial consideration. Some of the pieces would, as Vicky had said, fetch a good price…enough to pay for a fur coat, or a trip to Tenerife. But some of them had been favourites of his first wife, Angharad, whom Marissa inescapably resembled, and there was no gainsaying that his daughter had a claim, on sentimental grounds.

So he put off a decision, avoided making up his mind, fobbing off both women with half-promises which satisfied neither. The atmosphere at Grafton Court thickened palpably, and, far from having a peaceful convalescence, Marissa found the stress harder to bear than ever before.

She was tempted to cut her losses and run—go somewhere hot and lie on a beach for a month, mindlessly, turning brown and thinking of nothing. But then she remembered that these weeks leading up to the sale would be the last she would ever spend here. They were precious to her, in spite of all the difficulties, and she refused to be driven out prematurely.

She solved her problem by being alone as much as possible, taking solitary walks and rides—a little further each day, as the doctor had advised, spending a lot of time in the garden whenever it was fine enough to do so.

'Davy employs a jobbing gardener to do that sort of thing,' Vicky taunted one day, coming across Marissa weeding borders. 'Anyhow, what's the point, when the garden will be deep under builders' rubble before the summer is out?'

Marissa had always hated the way Vicky called her father 'Davy', a name that might be suitable for a man twenty years younger, but sounded odd applied to one of his mature years. Now she sat back on her heels and surveyed the other woman with a meagre satisfaction.

'No, it won't. Rick isn't going to pull down the house. He's going to turn it into a country house hotel.'

Vicky's face was contorted with conflicting emotions—angry because she had not known this first, yet eaten up with curiosity.

'He told you that himself?' she demanded. 'Well, well! And it's "Rick" all of a sudden, is it? The way you behaved at first, you had us all believing he was beneath contempt, but once you realised what an attractive man he was, you soon changed your tune, didn't you?'

Marissa smiled sweetly. 'Do you think he's attractive, Vicky? Better not let my father hear you saying so.'

She laughed and returned to attacking the weeds,

not troubling to deny her stepmother's allegations.
Let her believe, if she chose to, that Marissa and
Rick were friendly. Certainly the notion annoyed
her, for since Marissa had acquired a reputation as
a beauty, Vicky had looked on her as a rival for the
attention of every man who chanced by.

Glancing up, Marissa saw that she was alone
once more in the garden, which suited her just fine.

A week had elapsed since the day Rick had left
when her father and Vicky set off early in the
morning to go to Cheltenham. They were going to
view a likely property, Marissa knew. Vicky had
made sure she knew, although Davis had said
nothing directly. Even so, it was bliss to have the
house to herself for a whole day. Although it was
May, and the sun was shining, the wind was cool,
and it was pleasant to know she need not go out of
the house in search of solitude.

She pottered around, inspecting her mother's
collection of porcelain in its glass-fronted cabinet,
taking stock of the books on the study shelves,
wandering from room to room unhindered, secure
in the knowledge that she would not come across
Vicky in any of them. What I'm really doing is
saying goodbye to all of them, she thought
morbidly, and this cast a black shadow over the day.

In an only partially successful attempt to dispel
her sadness, she sat down at the piano in the
drawing-room and began to play idly. She did not
hear the doorbell and from this room was not able
to see the car approaching up the drive.

The first she saw of Rick Jablonski was when she
glanced up from her music to see him standing in
the doorway watching her, and the mixed quality of
her own reactions shocked her.

Surprise, yes, and an all too vivid recollection of the circumstances in which they had last parted, which made the colour drain further from the pale skin that rarely blushed. But there was something else—a leap of recognition, a reaching out, which she distrusted and quelled immediately.

'How did you get in?' she demanded.

'Your housekeeper opened the door. I told her I'd find you myself—it wasn't difficult. But don't stop playing.' He closed the door behind him and crossed the room; it seemed to take him no more than three strides.

Wild horses would not have dragged another note from Marissa, with him looking at her across the piano.

'I'm badly out of practice, I'm afraid.' She closed the lid firmly. 'I thought you were back in the States. You said...you said you had a plane to catch.'

'Planes go to other places. I've been in Europe—to Holland, France and Germany, looking at sites. All suitable, fortunately.'

To say she was glad would have demonstrated a generosity towards him she could not feel, so she merely nodded. Untroubled by her distinct lack of warmth, Rick said, 'I took a chance on finding you here alone, since your father and stepmother weren't at home.'

'How did *you* know that?' she asked quickly, suspiciously, and he grinned.

'From Gill at the Black Lion. Your village intelligence knocks the CIA into a cocked hat!'

'Of course. You can sneeze at one end, and someone will come running up from the other with a cold remedy,' Marissa said aggrievedly. 'You might have realised that they're now speculating on just why you wanted to see me alone—as I am myself.'

'You needn't worry. I know we left off at an interesting point, but I'm in no hurry to resume,' he told her.

She sniffed disdainfully, telling herself that the faint rebuff did not trouble her at all.

'That's just as well. I can scream good and loud enough to fetch Mrs Reed at a gallop, and then you'd really be a local scandal,' she said dismissively.

'That would be a pity, since what I really need is as much goodwill as I can drum up,' he said cheerfully. 'Which is where you come in. There's a small favour you can do me.'

Marissa did not even attempt to smother her gasp of half-amused astonishment.

'Me? Do *you* a favour? Give me one good reason why I should?' she cried.

'Because I'm saving Grafton Court from a fate worse than death,' he essayed lightly. 'There are worse things that could happen to it, you know. This way, it stays intact, and all the tenant farmers merely have a new landlord. Do you really want me to pull out and let in some rapacious developer?'

She laughed humourlessly.

'That's as loaded a question as "have you stopped beating your wife?",' she said scornfully. But her curiosity was aroused, despite herself. 'What is it you want me to do?'

'I'd like you to give a small dinner party on my behalf. Here. About a dozen people—yourself, your father, and Vicky included, naturally. Invite a few of the people who live locally, who you think I should meet, who are influential in forming opinion. I'm sure you know them all, and could do it beautifully.'

Marissa stood up, pushing back the piano stool in agitation. It was ironic! He was taking over Grafton Court, and he wanted *her*, of all people, to smooth the way for him! She was not stupid enough to think him naïve, so he must possess more naked audacity than ten of his peers put together! She would refuse—of course!

'You want *me* to act as hostess for you?' she said, shaking her dark head, still laughing. 'Oh, that's rich! Even coming from you, that's one of the best I've heard.' What I can't understand is why you haven't asked Vicky—I'm sure it would be right up her street, and she'd adore to do it.'

Rick eyed her shrewdly, waiting for her amusement to subside.

'I don't doubt she'd be only too delighted,' he agreed lightly. 'And that's the second good reason why *you* would do it. Wouldn't you say, Marissa?'

She could only stare at him, blank, beaten, knowing that he had her. Knowing herself outsmarted. For what he was planning was not so much a party as a wake, for all she had loved and held most dear. And she'd shoot herself before she'd let Vicky preside over that!

CHAPTER FOUR

VICKY was briefly incensed when she learned of the task Rick had set Marissa.

'He's what? But that's preposterous!' she cried. '*I'm* the mistress of this house, and if there's any entertaining to be done, then *I* should be the one to arrange it!'

Marissa only smiled. Vicky had had such a high opinion of Rick, as the putative buyer of Grafton Court; it wouldn't hurt for him to come down a little in her estimation. But after he phoned her one day, she seemed somewhat mollified.

'I do believe Rick thinks involving Marissa in this way will reconcile her to what has to happen,' Marissa heard her saying to Davis.

If that's really what he thinks, he's way off beam, she thought indignantly. But the truth was considerably more complex.

'The secret of management is in choosing the right man—or woman—for the job. Pegs for slots,' he told her briskly, with a wry smile. 'In my opinion, this is one for you. You've lived all your life in this area, known people around here since childhood. I reckon you'd be a more...' he hesitated '...a more tactful hostess.'

Marissa sniffed.

'That's not the version you handed out to Vicky.'

'It would be pointless—and foolish—of me to

offend her unnecessarily,' he said. 'That's not good business either. Don't you know anything, Marissa?'

'I know a first-class con artist when I meet one,' she retorted. 'What makes you so sure I won't deliberately sabotage the affair—invite people who haven't spoken to each other for years, devise a positively ghastly menu, and ensure that the whole thing is a complete fiasco!'

A giggle escaped her at the thought of icy silence around the dining table, cold soup, sloppy service, the important event degenerating into mild chaos. But Rick merely shot an approving glance in her direction.

'You look completely different when you laugh—I mean really laugh, not that Mona Lisa smile you save for *Elle*, he remarked. More intently, he continued, 'Shall I tell you why I trust you implicitly not to engineer a débâcle? Because you wouldn't lower yourself to let down the noble reputation of Grafton Court at this late stage—however much you might want to. Your dinner party will be a success if it kills you, and you'll smile and be charming, even while you're hating every minute. So get working on that guest list, Marissa. I want this thing arranged during June, just before the sale goes through.'

Marissa was so consumed with loathing for him at that moment that only the memory of his raw power and strength, his swift propensity for anger, restrained her from springing at him. It did not help, either, that she knew he was right. She'd bring this party off brilliantly, at whatever cost to herself.

She went home immediately and consulted Mrs Reed, and a very superior catering company who would supply extra staff to help cook and serve.

So far, so good. There would be herself, Davis and Vicky—and Rick, of course. She had already asked him whether he wished to bring a guest, and he'd favoured her with his slow. ambiguous smile. 'Why, no, Marissa. I shall expect you to be my partner. So don't invite your boyfriend and foul up the numbers.'

Marissa, who had a steady flow of young men who asked her out on dates, would have been hard put to it to find anyone who answered to that description. She was too busy, too rarely in one place, she told herself, but in reality the only man she had ever fallen for, long ago when she first took up modelling, had let her down so badly that she had been wary of too-deep involvement ever since. But she was not of a mind to confide this to Rick Jablonski, who would probably find it funny—or store up the knowledge to use, in some way, as ammunition against her. It didn't do, where he was concerned, to leave any visible chinks in one's personal armour.

'I class this as business, and therefore won't attempt to mix pleasure with it,' she told him shortly, anticipating, all the same, how very odd it would feel to go in to dinner on this man's arm. By doing so, she knew, she would appear to be tacitly sanctioning his takeover, but what else could she do? He had very smartly and slyly manoeuvred her into a corner from which she could not escape.

So, back to her list. She invited Dr Pritchard, who accepted delightedly and said he would bring along his daughter who would be visiting him at the time, the vicar of Bishopswell and his wife, the local Member of Parliament and his. The most prosperous and influential of their tenant farmers, together with his widowed sister who kept house for him, made up a good representative dozen, she decided with satisfaction.

Lurking at the back of her mind was a malicious little demon of hope that at least one of these people would find Rick antipathetic, that he would put someone's back up, that one or more of her guests would be less than totally charmed by him. He, of course, would be out to ensure that did not happen, and it would be interesting to watch him pick his way through this minefield of diverse personalities.

The dinner was arranged for the first Saturday evening in June. Davis was delighted to see his daughter so totally absorbed in the preparations, issuing invitations, ordering flowers, doing her utmost to make sure that the house looked its immaculate best for the occasion.

'It's nice to see that you've come round a little,' he remarked with satisfaction. 'I knew you'd realise that Jablonski wasn't such a villain, once you got to know him.'

'I have done nothing of the kind, and I prefer to reserve judgement about Rick Jablonski,' she replied in level tones. 'However, having undertaken to assist with this public relations exercise of his, I feel morally obliged to ensure it all goes smoothly.'

'And I'm sure it will. You remind me of your mother,' be observed, with a half-smile. 'Dreamy, she was, most of the time, drifting about the place, wrapped up in her music, or out with the horses, but when we entertained, a transformation took place. Snap—she was all bright-eyed efficiency.'

It was a long time since he had spoken of his first wife, and Marissa was absurdly gratified to know that she wasn't entirely forgotten. So, although she wondered how her mother would have reacted to this parting of the ways, she forbore to voice her thoughts aloud.

There's nothing in this for me, she mused bitterly, except the personal satisfaction of not making a fool of myself in front of Rick Jablonski, of proving that I can accomplish what I set out to do. I don't give twopence for his approval, anyhow, but I don't want him sneering at me. Or Vicky either. She would be only too overjoyed if it were a resounding failure and the fault could be laid at my door.

At least the day dawned fine, much to her relief, and the weather forecast promised that it would remain so. Sunshine and the assurance of a calm, warm evening made her feel more sanguine, as if the elements were on her side. The flowers arrived and she supplemented them with more from the garden, arranging them artistically in the hall and dining-room. On the great oak table, the Georgian silver épergne swam in its own polished reflection, along with the elegant silver cutlery and the scintillating Bohemian glassware. Marissa personally inspected every place setting, after casting an approving eye over the shining wood floors and sparkling windows, where Mrs Reed's team had worked like willing slaves.

'They won't find a mark anywhere, Miss Marissa,' that lady had assured her, with taut satisfaction. 'They won't eat better salmon, either, than the one Jed brought me this morning.'

Marissa smiled. She had her own suspicions as to where Jed obtained his salmon—poaching on Beaumont land was a long tradition in his family. But the fish was a beauty, and she wasn't going to quibble about its origins today.

Vicky had been to the hairdresser that afternoon, and returned with her blonde curls upswept and strongly redolent of hairspray. She'd bought a new dress, too, earlier in the week, from an expensive boutique in Gloucester, hidden it away and allowed no one to see it before today.

Marissa herself had been far too busy for shopping, and had in any event made up her mind what she was going to wear. The guests were due to arrive at eight, and she knew she had left herself very little time in which to get ready. But this was her forte, and she was used to working quickly and under pressure with the raw material at her disposal—herself. Mouth full of grips, she pinned her hair up on top of her head, allowing one thick, glossy dark plait to fall smoothly from the centre to the nape of her slim neck, emphasising its length. Skilful use of blusher heightened her cheekbones and the wide purity of her brow, from which all her hair was severely swept back. Her dress was a plain swathe of scarlet silk, cut like a cheongsam, with a prim, high, unrevealing neckline. She was totally covered, almost puritanical, except that when she moved one saw that the skirt was slit from ankle to mid-thigh, revealing occasional glimpses of smooth, tanned leg.

She did hope it would not shock the vicar—her legs would, after all, be under the table most of the time. Certainly it wouldn't scandalise Dr Pritchard, who had delivered her and treated most of her childhood ailments, or Brian Jenkins, with whose son and daughter she had climbed trees and run wild as a teenage tomboy. As for Anthony Fielding, MP, an erstwhile polytechnic lecturer, still in his thirties, she was sure he'd seen more revealing outfits on his students, if not in the House of Commons!

So for whose benefit was the siren-coloured dress with the slashed skirt? Surely she wasn't wearing it to impress Rick Jablonski, who had carried her unconscious into this very house, teased her, taunted her, misled her…at least implicitly…as to his intentions about Grafton Court, and kissed her savagely when she'd dared fight back with whatever weapons came to hand. Surely not?

She met her stepmother at the top of the staircase. Vicky was in a pink and blue flowered silk dress which bared her arms and a fair amount of creamy décolletage, but, looking Marissa up and down, she commented unblushingly, 'It's a bit…well, revealing, isn't it?'

Marissa laughed.

'Perhaps, but at the dinner table I reckon they'll see more of *you* than they do of me,' she retorted cheerfully, and they descended the stairs together in silence.

Davis and Rick were already in the Hall, having a drink. It was the first time Marissa had seen the American in a dark, formal suit, and her breath was taken away, as if a force nine gale had hit her full in the chest. Nothing could disguise the breadth of those shoulders, or the power of that tall physique, but the buccaneering general had been subtly transformed into a splendid, half-savage nobleman, the gilt-fair hair brushed back into shining obedience from the firm brow, beneath which the clear, slightly mocking sea-green eyes regarded her directly. Their gaze was both approving and adversorial. Here I am—here you are. You've got everything it takes, but I can more than match you, it challenged.

Her taunt came back to disturb her. He didn't look in the least like a peasant. He looked as if he had been born to wear a dinner suit and move easily and with assurance among people from all walks of life. But didn't that kind of unconscious arrogance have to be bred in over the generations? It had to be an illusion, she told herself. He'd made no secret of his background.

The odd fluttering sensation below her heart slowly stabilised as she forced herself to inhale deeply but carefully.

'Well now,' Rick said quietly, under cover of handing her a drink, 'that's some dress. It gives a whole new meaning to biology, just watching you move.'

Starting, not as she would have expected, from her face, but from a point near her ankle, his examination of her slowly traversed her half-bared leg, inching upwards to the smooth curve of her breasts beneath the red silk. 'I don't know what's more enticing—what I can see, or what I can only imagine.'

Marissa did not turn away or lower her eyes, but remained still, not submitting to his scrutiny, but enduring it, and something strange happened to her. For many years her body had been simply a tool of her trade, studied, posed and photographed and directed, and she had so regarded it herself. Many men had looked at it, some with desire, some with professional detachment and she had remained undisturbed by both.

But now, under this man's cool gaze, she was deeply aware of the beginnings of a wayward excitement, a fierce, secret exultation in her own beauty and its power. It was as if the dress, having first seized his attention, had melted away, and his eyes were exploring her nakedness...and she was taking pleasure in his admiration, soaking it up like a sponge, rejoicing in it...

That's disgusting! she thought furiously, giving herself a little inward shake.

'Rick, I've done all I can to make this evening a success,' she said coldly. 'I'm not sure what point you're trying to score by embarrassing me.'

'Embarrassing you? For goodness's sake——' He laughed, low but harshly. 'That was a compliment, woman! And surely one you were prepared for? You're hardly dressed to disappear into the wallpaper, are you?'

He dropped the subject there, leaving Marissa to reflect that she had got no more than she deserved. He had an alarming tendency to say just what he thought—but then she had known that all along. It was a relief to glance out of the window and see the first of the guests arriving!

Blessedly, then, she was too busy to monopolise his attention, and he, she realised, was too busy to favour her with it. She had been no more than an hors-d'oeuvre, to whet his appetite, and now she was obliged to watch with rueful admiration as the powerful business machine that was Rick Jablonski swung effortlessly into action.

Every one of the people here tonight had known the Beaumonts for some years—many years, in some cases. To most of them, this family and the land it had inherited were synonymous. It must have been with a sense of shock that they had heard that Davis Beaumont was obliged to sell, ending a centuries-old tradition, and it would have been surprising if there had not been an undercurrent of suspicion, even of resentment, towards the man who was ending it. An outsider—a foreigner, even. They must have heard the rumours about him—a self-made man who had thrashed his way to wealth and prominence—and expected him to be brash and unsympathetic.

As he is, Marissa thought uncharitably. But Rick had done his homework, and that was not the way he came across tonight. He knew...or had made it his task to learn...something about each of his fellow guests.

Marissa, supervising the catering staff as they circulated with the drinks, heard him telling the vicar that he had a cousin in the priesthood, and a lively, amiable discussion about ecumenism followed. With Anthony Fielding he talked about the differences between the English and the American political systems, and to Brian Jenkins he revealed that his Polish ancestors had worked on the land, years ago. Were they tenant farmers too? Not exactly, said Rick, with a wry grin.

When Marissa caught up with him, he was deep in conversation with Dr Pritchard and his daughter Ruth, a dark, intelligent young woman in her early thirties, who was no one's fool. But she was smiling too, and obviously enjoyed crossing mental swords with this interesting stranger.

'My, my—even our Ruthie is captivated,' Vicky murmured maliciously in her stepdaughter's ear. 'Not that she has a snowball's chance in hell of snaring Rick. Nowhere near pretty enough, and besides, money tends to marry money.'

Marissa looked sharply at her. 'Ruth is very

attractive, in her own way, and smart too. The fact
that she's single doesn't mean no one has asked
her,' she said. 'Maybe she prefers it that way.'

'Codswallop, dear,' Vicky said sweetly. 'Every
woman needs a man, whether she admits it or not.
Even you. I bet you wouldn't put up too much of a
fight if our hero there lusted after you. Or perhaps
he already has?'

Marissa kept her smile fixed on her face.

'Don't be crude,' she said. Catching Mrs Reed's
eye, she received the signal that dinner was about
to be served, and escaped gratefully. Vicky's hints
recalled all too easily the feelings which had
troubled her earlier, and she was fiercely reluctant
to admit to finding Rick physically attractive. It was
morally indefensible to dislike and resent a man,
and yet fantasise about him making love to her, she
was guiltily convinced.

She did not tighten her hand over his sleeve as
they led the guests in to dinner. Nor did she have
to, to feel the hard bulk of muscle beneath her
fingers, the warm, pervasive brush of his leg
against her thigh. Alarm coursed through her. If she
could be so disturbed by a casual, meaningless
touch, how would she react if he touched her with
deliberate sexual intent? I'll never find out, she
vowed fervently.

Marissa too had done her homework. Leafing
through cookery books, she'd discovered that cold
fruit soups were a Polish speciality, and so for the
first course she had served one made with wine and
figs. Rick smiled appreciatively as he caught her
eye, and now, foolishly, she *did* look away,
disconcerted by his pleasure.

The dinner itself was a triumph, and compliments

flowed around the table. The salmon was excellent, the crown roast of lamb succulently cooked and presented with young summer vegetables, the wines superbly chosen. The service was quiet, efficient and unobtrusive, and nothing went wrong. Nor were there any overt conversational gaffes, so far as Marissa was aware. She allowed herself a small sigh of satisfied relief as everyone disposed of crêpes wrapped delicately around a rum-soaked ice-cream confection.

'Wonderful dinner, Davis,' Brian Jenkins said admiringly. Marissa smiled to herself as her father accepted the praise, everyone else joining in and adding to it.

'It was indeed,' Rick agreed unhesitatingly. 'However, we mustn't forget that the organisational genius behind it was Marissa's.'

He raised his glass, looking directly at her, but the length of the table separated them, and she could not make out the expression in his eyes. Was he trying to embarrass her yet again? If so, he had succeeded brilliantly. She looked down the table as everyone else's glass was raised too, but could not help encountering Vicky's false, brilliant smile.

The cheese board had circulated, and everyone was drinking brandy and liqueurs when Rick briefly held up his hand and requested silence. Miraculously, the table fell quiet at once, everyone's eyes fixed expectantly on him.

'I asked Marissa to arrange this little get-together tonight so that I could meet you all, get to know you some, and allay a few of the misgivings I know you must be feeling.'

There was a brief ripple of dissent, no one wanting to admit to harbouring dark suspicions about a man who had been so charming and friendly to them for the past couple of hours. But he shook his head.

'No—really. It would be surprising, and unnatural, if you hadn't had your doubts. You don't know me, and I'm sure you've heard all kinds of rumours, some less pleasant than others.'

He paused, and one or two people laughed faintly, as if to deny that they either indulged in or listened to such gossip. Marissa sat stock-still. She had said not a word to anyone outside this house, but still, she could not help feeling a slight, irrational guilt. She, more than anyone, had condemned him virtually unheard.

Rick looked slowly around his audience, all of whom were sitting very quietly, held, as it were, in the palm of his hand. He has them, Marissa thought, torn between disgust and admiration. They're already half-way to accepting him, believing in his goodwill towards them. All it needed was time, and a careful, unhurried approach, and if he was prepared to give them that, he was home and dry.

Favouring them all with his slow, easy smile, he said, 'I know you're going to miss the Beaumont family, and there's no way a newcomer like myself could ever take their place. But if you'll accept me as your neighbour, I'll do my best to be a good one.'

An air of puzzlement hung over the table, a miasma of mystery, deliberately induced.

It was Dr Pritchard who asked quietly, 'Mr Jablonski, correct me if I've jumped to the wrong conclusion, but…do I understand that you are planning to *live* here at Grafton Court?'

'That's right,' Rick said cheerfully, tossing back the remains of his brandy.

The table erupted into a babble of questions and exclamations. Marissa, as still and silent as if shock had turned her to stone, saw her stepmother's mouth fall slowly open.

'But, Rick,' said Vicky, 'I thought you were going to turn Grafton Court into a hotel. That's what Marissa told me,' she added accusingly, glaring across the table at the dumbstruck girl.

Everyone's eyes were on Marissa now, and the ice in her veins quickly turned to the molten lava of angry embarrassment. He'd spun her a fine story, bamboozled her into believing it. She'd passed it on to Vicky, as he must have known she'd be unable to resist doing, and Vicky, of course, had circulated it around the entire neighbourhood. But now it was she, Marissa, who came across as the prize idiot for having got hold of the wrong end of the stick.

She wasn't about to sit tamely under this treatment.

'You move too quickly for me to keep pace with you, Rick,' she said sweetly, the smile on her lips failing to reach her eyes. 'First of all, we're going to have a leisure park, then a country house hotel, then—abracadabra! You've decided to play the country squire instead! Are you normally this indecisive?'

His gaze fixed on her across the table, cutting across the space between them.

'I'm *never* indecisive,' he told her firmly. 'Grafton Court was never going to be a leisure park, as I explained to you—the area isn't suitable. I did think it would make a good hotel, but that was *before* my trip to Europe. When I realised how heavily committed I'm going to be over here for the next few years, I realised I'm going to need a home base. I can't live forever out of suitcases.'

Marissa was so stunned by what she had just learned that she all but missed Mrs Reed's frantic signal that coffee was ready to be served in the drawing-room. Weakly she rose to her feet and led the company, still agog from the news, out of the dining-room.

It was, she realised, a brilliantly engineered coup.

First Rick had softened them up, leading them to believe that he wasn't so bad, and that what he had in mind was at least bearable. Then, when he startlingly divulged that he intended to become their neighbour, they were pleased, relieved—flattered, even.

As they sat drinking coffee in the drawing-room, Marissa heard the vicar's wife giving him a brief, potted guide to the area, and all she thought he would need to know.

'Your wife will find there are quite good shopping centres within thirty miles or so,' she said encouragingly. 'I except she'll have her own car.'

'Mr Jablonski isn't married, dear,' her husband reminded her.

'Oh. What a pity,' she remarked, looking at Rick sympathetically, as if she'd just learned he had some awful affliction. He would be bombarded with invitations to Sunday lunch at the vicarage, Marissa thought wryly.

And then, on the pretext of thanking Mrs Reed and her staff, she had to leave the room. It came over her with all the ferocity of delayed shock reaction that Rick Jablonski would be living here, in her beloved home, in a few short weeks' time—when she had left it forever. He would walk in the grounds, eat, sleep, and do...well, whatever else he did...in these very rooms. Grafton Court would be his, his, his!

Feeling ill and drained again, she leaned her head against the wall of the corridor, asking herself vainly just what it was that she wanted of him. He wasn't going to pull down the house, tear up the land, or convert it for wealthy visitors to enjoy. He was going to make it his 'home base' as he termed it, and still she wasn't happy, wasn't satisfied. Because whatever he planned involved her leaving, never to return. Tears welled in her eyes, making her mascara run and sting, and she was obliged to dodge into the cloakroom to effect repairs. No one must see her in this state—him least of all!

Pulling herself together, she went to the kitchen and congratulated everyone on a superb evening's work, praising them unstintingly for their efforts. She knew she should return to her guests, but didn't feel she could summon the strength, right away, so she slipped out into the blessed peace of the garden.

The faintest breeze stirred the branches of the old apple trees, enfolding her in a cloud of heady blossom-scent. The brilliant moonlight blanched the white walls so that they stood out starkly against the contrasting blackness of the wooden beams. It picked out, too, the white shirt front and bright hair of the man picking his way across the orchard towards her, and she was struck anew by the strange regality of his bearing.

She didn't move.

'What are you doing out here, Rick?' she asked woodenly.

'Oddly enough, I came to see what *you* were doing. And to bring you back inside. You're the hostess, and I'm the host, in a sense, so it's going to look mighty odd if we're both skulking in the garden. What *will* people think?'

Marissa shook her head, too weak and spent to cope with his teasing.

'Leave me alone, Rick. You've had your pound of flesh from me tonight. Give me a little space.'

He placed a hand on the bough of a tree, just above her head, and tested his weight against it.

'You don't like the idea of my living here? Even though I undertake to retain all the estate staff, and ensure tenure for all the farmers? Damn it, I'll even take on the horses and give them a home, if it will make you happy!' He looked down at her, his face etched in hard lines. 'But it won't, will it? Yours is a dog-in-the-manger attitude. What *you* can't have, no one should.'

A tremor ran through her, and she couldn't say that his accusation was entirely unfounded. 'You had your mind made up when you came to see me that day, hadn't you? Possibly even before. But you didn't tell me. You used me to prepare the ground for you, to make things easier…and you kept me in the dark!'

He shrugged.

'I wanted to see how you would acquit yourself.'

'Really? How many did I score?' she flung at him. 'Do I deserve a B-plus?'

'Oh, better than that,' he said softly. 'You were a perfect hostess, Marissa. The evening was a brilliant success, just as I desired. In fact, we made a first-rate team.'

She turned her head away, saying bitterly, 'Team? You conned me into it! Go away, Rick—I hate you, I hate myself, and right now——' her voice was thick with angry tears '—I hate the entire world!'

His large, powerful hand forced her chin round so that she was obliged to look at him.

'No, you don't, Marissa. Right now you feel foolish and full of self-pity, but that will pass,' he said firmly. 'It doesn't take a genius to see that you're not at all fit. What's more, you think your world has come to an end, and that you'll have to leave here, but it doesn't have to be that way.'

More confused than ever, she stared up at him. 'I don't understand.'

'You will,' he promised her. 'Put a smile on your face, and come back inside. You're agitated and overwrought, and I won't throw any more at you tonight. Have lunch with me tomorrow, and I'll explain. OK?'

And, leaning forward, he kissed her just once, very gently, on the mouth, disturbing her with his unexpected tenderness, before taking her hand and leading her back into the house.

CHAPTER FIVE

RICK WAS right when he had said she could take in no more that night. Once the guests had left Marissa, too numb to feel anything, peeled off her clothes, fell into bed, and knew nothing more until morning.

But on waking, her first thought was that she had agreed to meet Rick for lunch, and at once her senses were alert. Ever since she had met him, he had feinted one blow and felled her with another, and now she no longer knew which way to tread to be safe with him. She trusted him no more today than she had in the beginning, and was half inclined to cancel the appointment, but curiosity impelled her onwards.

A way in which she did not have to leave Grafton Court? Was he planning to rent part of it off to her? There were a couple of cottages on the estate not occupied, she knew. Perhaps it would appeal to his twisted sense of humour to turn out the former daughter of the house and keep her on as his tenant.

'Where shall I meet you tomorrow?' she had asked him last night, just before he left.

'I'll pick you up. Eleven-thirty prompt,' he had replied unhelpfully, and she had let out a sigh.

'Rick! If I don't know where you're taking me, how do I know what to wear?' she had demanded in exasperation.

He had merely grinned, said, 'Don't overdress,' and left it at that. Marissa assumed he meant a country pub as opposed to a smart restaurant in Hereford or Gloucester, and so she wore fine babycord trousers, a silk shirt and a knitted jacket. Even so, she was surprised when he turned up in denims and a sweatshirt, looking more like a PE instructor than a property tycoon, glanced quickly down at her canvas brogues and said, 'I suppose they'll do.'

'Just where *are* we going?' she queried as he started the car.

'Them as asks no questions isn't told no lies,' he replied mysteriously. He drove only a few miles before turning off the road, down a narrow track which led down to the banks of the River Wye, where willows screened a small, shingly beach.

Marissa watched as he opened the boot, took out a rug, and spread it on the ground. A hamper was next, followed by a large cardboard box which he proceeded to open.

She laughed unable to hide a cry of pleasure.

'It's a barbecue!'

'Sure is. I'm a sucker for the great outdoors,' Rick agreed. 'And since this ain't California, we have to grab the good weather while we can. Come on—don't just stand there. Help me set up this thing.'

'Rick, this has never even been used,' she said slowly, fingering the shiny metal grid.

'Hardly, since I bought it this very morning,' he admitted, ripping open a bag of charcoal and scattering a layer in the pan. 'Tell you what—I'll get the fire going, you open some wine. We can't cook the steaks until the coals are red.'

Marissa fished in the hamper, drew out a bottle of excellent claret, and uncorked it. She felt, all of a sudden, absurdly young and light hearted, and, if she did not altogether forget it, she put out of her mind whatever purpose lay behind the invitation. This was like playtime. The fire was smoking nicely, the sun was shining, and Rick, tongs in one hand, had a boyish grin on his face and a black smudge on his forehead.

She knelt on the rug and poured two glasses of wine. Setting down the tongs, he flung himself carelessly down at her side, taking the glass from her hand.

'*Na zdrowie*,' he said, tossing back the contents briskly.

She laughed. 'You don't do anything by halves, do you? And what was that you said?'

'*Na zdrowie*? It means, to your very good health, or, more loosely translated, "cheers",' he said. Frowning a little, he added, 'It's not an affectation. I was brought up speaking Polish all the time at home, and sometimes it still slips out instinctively. I was christened "Ryszard" and my family don't call me Rick, but "Ryszek".'

'Ryszek—I like that,' she said, and fishing out a paper napkin from the hamper, 'Hold still—you've branded yourself with the tongs.'

It was a mistake, she realised, as she scrubbed ineffectively at the smudge on his face, for it brought her closer to him than she had ever intended. He took hold of her wrist, the napkin fluttered unheeded to the rug, and then he was kissing her, not roughly and punitively, as he had that day in the car, but slowly, exploratively, tasting and savouring her. She sucked in her breath; only last night she had wondered how it would feel to be touched by him, and now his mouth was on hers, and it was dizzingly sweet.

But they each had a glass in one hand, the fire crackled warningly behind them, and Rick drew away, leaving her aching with a dissatisfaction she had never known before. Because she knew he could have gone further, without any objections from her, and yet he had not. Whatever he had brought her here for, it could not have been to try and make love to her, for he had just turned his back on his best chance.

He didn't allude to it at all, simply treated the moment as something that had happened, and been put behind him, slapping the steaks on the hot grid and flipping them over expertly as they sizzled.

Marissa tried to follow his casual example—a kiss was nothing, these days—and busied herself taking salad, bread rolls, cheese and fruit from the hamper.

It all tasted delicious, eaten in the fresh air, with the river only a few feet away, and birds warbling and squawking in the trees behind them. Rick boiled water in a small pan over the still hot coals, and made coffee, and they leaned back, side by side, for once at ease and companionable with one another.

'Don't you have any corporate plans to hatch today?' Marissa asked teasingly. 'No deals to make, no properties to take over? Is the great Jablonski actually skiving?'

'Skiving?' He frowned.

'Bunking off. Playing truant,' she translated with a grin. 'Who coined that saying about two peoples divided by a common language?'

'Whoever it was had a point,' he observed. 'But as a matter of fact I'm hard at work, right now, filling a vital appointment. A position where a wrong choice could be disastrous.'

Marissa sat up, all the light-heartedness draining from her. Of course, he hadn't brought her here just for fun, she should have remembered. He was up to something—wasn't he always? Something that concerned her, and what troubled her most was that she was several steps behind him, not understanding how his mind was working, only knowing that it *was*, and that she should beware.

'I don't know what you're talking about,' she said carefully.

Rick picked up a stick and, still lolling easily, scratched a rough pattern on the ground.

'Marissa, hasn't it ever occurred to you that a model's career is limited to a few youthful years? Haven't you ever thought about what you're going to do with the time that's left? The rest of your life?'

She started.

'Occasionally,' she admitted cautiously. 'But I'm not over the hill yet. I think I have a few more years before I need worry about the crows' feet and the wrinkles!'

'Undoubtedly. By which time, I suppose, you assume that some red-blooded male will have snapped you up and married you?'

'To be strictly truthful, I haven't exactly banked on marriage as an alternative career,' she said. 'It *could* happen, but then again, it might not. What I mean is, there's no one I feel that way about, right now.'

'Hm.' He was thoughtful. 'You know, I meant what I said last night about making Grafton Court my home. I'm going to be expanding rapidly into Europe, and living over here for some years, so it makes sense to have somewhere permanent.'

'I suppose so.' Marissa didn't see the connection, but already knew Rick well enough to be sure that there was one, and if he wanted her to know, he would tell her. There was no need to fish.

The stick scratched busily for a few seconds, then came to rest again.

'Also, it seems to me that things are conducted differently over here. There's less business done in the office, more over the dinner table. Colleagues and potential partners are invited home. One becomes part of a community. The social side is important, and can't be neglected.'

'So you need a nice country house to bring your buddies home for weekends—shooting parties and drinkies and all the trimmings,' she said, mock-flippantly. 'Well, Grafton Court should serve that purpose well, Rick. It has just about everything.'

'*Just about*,' he repeated meaningfully. 'You hit the nail squarely on the head there, Marissa. Oh, I know there's Mrs Reed and her helpers, but a man in my position, who has a lot of entertaining to do, needs a hostess... someone to organise and smooth the path...to lend grace to the scene. You showed, last night, how well you fulfilled that role. Charming, beautiful, well-bred, efficient...all the adjectives fit. Grafton Court needs you, Marissa. And, if I'm going to live there, so do I.'

Every breath she took was painfully fought for, drawn along airways that were squeezed tight by emotion.

'So that's what all this is about,' she forced

herself to answer him. 'You're offering me a job—a cross between housekeeper and social secretary? You want me to live in my own home, as an employee, and you think I'm so desperate to stay here that I'll give up a lucrative career to do so?' She paused, but only for long enough to recover her breath. 'Well, let me tell you, Rick, that even if you were to match my earnings to the last penny, you could never pay me enough!'

Her eyes were dark and enormous in a face white with angry humiliation, and she could feel her entire body quivering uncontrollably. How dared he demean her this way! And he still lay back on his elbows, watching her as if she were performing a play, quite unworried and casual, with a smile on his face. And still playing idly with that wretched stick!

'I wasn't planning on paying you, Marissa —not directly, although you'd certainly be a very rich lady,' he said. 'I suppose you could say I was offering you a job, but only in the most loose sense of the word. I've never done this before, so don't blame me for making an utter hash of it, but I was asking you if you would consider being my wife.'

Marissa sat back, hands clenched on her knees, tense with incredulity. He had to be joking—this had to be some stupid, ridiculous hoax at her expense! But he wasn't laughing, his face was perfectly serious, although quite calm, as if he had indeed offered her a job, without anything emotional involved in the transaction.

'You're mad!' she exclaimed. 'Why would I marry *you*, of all people? And why should you want me to?'

Rick shrugged.

'The equation is obvious. As my wife, you'd get to keep Grafton Court. It would be yours. As for me—well, as I said, you're very suitable. You go with the house. I've reached the stage where I should have a wife. All the people I deal with have them, and life is more conveniently arranged in couples. Like you, I don't have anyone poised to fill the part, nor do I have time and energy to spare hunting for one in the usual way.'

Marissa still could not take this crazy, unexpected proposal seriously.

'But, Rick,' she protested, 'the whole idea is preposterous! You don't...you don't love me,' she snatched desperately at the most conventional reason.

'You don't love *me* either. It's ideal. We're a matched pair,' he said equably. 'Don't you see, Marissa? I'm ambitious, and going places, but I'm an American, from who knows where, an adventurer. Can I be trusted? Am I acceptable? Of course I am, because I have a beautiful, stylish European wife, whose family have lived in our historic country house for centuries. Who could doubt my credentials? It's just perfect.'

He reached for the second bottle of wine and refilled both their glasses.

'Here—you look as though you need this,' he said with a grin.

'I certainly do. You've knocked me for six!' she exclaimed, and, when he looked suitably blank, she added, 'It's a cricketing expression. It means you've demolished my defences.'

'You see how much I have to learn? Every time I open my mouth, I'm liable to put my foot right in it.' he said woefully. 'Dammit, I can't even converse with the natives! And that's only English! I don't speak French either, but I'll bet *you* do!'

Marissa was laughing now, a slightly hysterical amusement compounded of wine and astonishment.

'Of course I do, fluently. I went to a very good school,' she told him. 'But you seem to have done all right for yourself so far, without someone like me to hold your hand.'

'I'll do all right—whatever,' said Rick, and behind the jauntiness she suddenly glimpsed the determination in the face of uncertainty of the man who had pulled himself up from nowhere. 'But it's time I was married, and you'll suit my image.'

'Rick, I can't marry you as part of a promotional package—it's a little more serious than arranging a dinner party,' she said soberly. 'You're holding out a very desirable carrot, but it just wouldn't be right for me to accept on those terms.'

'What's right or wrong?' he queried challengingly. 'It's only the way it seems to *us*, applies to *us*—we're not tied by anyone else's standard or conventions. In the past, our ancestors married for all kinds of reasons—financial, dynastic, or simply because they were ordered to do so. Love was the very least of it, and it was probably better that way. I don't want, or need, a heavy emotional involvement. Do you?'

She had a sudden, frightening vision of how it would be to love this dangerous, unpredictable adventurer, to be at his mercy emotionally.

'No!' she said swiftly, fervently.

'There you are, then. The defence rests,' he said. She was silent for a while, her expressive face troubled, and he said, 'Don't say any more right now. Let's enjoy the rest of our picnic. I shall be going to London tomorrow, and shan't be back until Thursday. I won't phone you, or write, or repeat what I've said, between now and then, but when I get back I shall want an answer.'

'Just like that?' she said.

'What do you mean, "just like that"? Hell, you'll have had three whole days.' He smiled, with just a hint of impatience. 'Have some more wine—I'm not throwing good claret to the fishes!'

On Monday, Marissa was quite sure that her answer would have to be an unequivocal "no". She couldn't marry any man for reasons other than love, and certainly not one she wasn't even sure she liked, half the time. Even if he was challenging and interesting, and sometimes fun to be with! The whole idea was ludicrous.

Then on Tuesday afternoon her father and Vicky came back from another visit to Cheltenham, announcing that they had agreed on the purchase of the property there, and were ready to proceed.

'But it's all going to take time, surely?' Marissa asked nervously.

'Not at all. Everything is straightforward on the purchase, and the contracts on the sale are signed and ready for exchanging,' Davis said brightly. 'Rick wants vacant possession by the middle of July, and I'm prepared to go along with that, even if it means Vicky and I have to rent somewhere until our house is ready.'

That was only a little more than a month! From something painful and unbearable, but nebulously in the future, this dreaded fall of the axe had acquired an awful imminence. Marissa was going to lose her home forever, she was going to be deeply and irreparably hurt, she was going to suffer an irreplaceable loss—soon. Very, very soon. So soon that she could almost hear the minutes ticking away on the clock.

'I do hope you've made some arrangements, Marissa,' said Vicky, on Wednesday morning. 'You won't be able to stay with Davy and me, not to begin with. I suppose there's always your flat, although London can be hell in summer.'

Vicky must know that she was nowhere near recovered enough to return to London and her job! If only she didn't have the uncomfortable but quite undeniable feeling that the part her stepmother was enjoying the most, in all this, was her own unhappiness, Marissa thought, pouring herself more tea and gazing miserably out of the window. The sun shone brightly, heartbreakingly, on the familiar gardens and the fields and hills beyond, every step of which was so achingly dear to her that she could scarcely contemplate not being able to sit here and gaze at this view. Never again. And she had thought it had hurt her to go away, at seventeen—that was nothing, nothing, compared to the incredible agony of this.

It doesn't *have* to be that way, a small voice whispered to her, half-way through Wednesday afternoon. You don't have to leave—not now, not ever. You can stay here and be Mrs Ryszard Jablonski. All right, you don't love him. But you aren't in love with anyone else, and who knows if you ever will be? Look on it as a job, one for which you're eminently trained and qualified. All your life, your education, to say nothing of years of breeding behind you, have equipped you to be the mistress of Grafton Court.

But not to be the wife of someone like Rick Jablonski, she protested, and the voice retorted wickedly, Why not? Come on now, what exactly does he want? Someone to arrange dinner parties and weekends, to be gracious and welcoming to his business colleagues. No problem. Someone to appear at his side at any function which demands a consort, to look good and smile nicely—you've spent years learning to do just that, and you're pretty well expert at it. He'll be away a lot, and even when he's home he'll be more involved with his empire-building than he'll ever be with you. It won't be too onerous. A lot of women would sell their souls for a rich, dynamic, good-looking husband like that!

She could not help feeling that if she married him that was precisely what she would be doing. Selling not just her soul, but the rest of her, to a bidder who was holding out the one thing she wanted, and could not otherwise have, in exchange. And no matter what that treacherously tempting little voice said, it would be no easy option. You couldn't be married to Rick Jablonski without belonging to him, being owned by him, and being aware of him, all the time.

Restless, confused, she put on firm shoes and tramped the estate, fighting herself, and losing, gradually, the will to refuse this strange bargain he had put to her. She climbed, with considerable effort, to the highest part of the Beaumont estate, which had always been known as Sheep Hill, from where in one direction one could see clear to the Black Mountains, and in the other to the smooth sweep of the Malverns. All this Rick was offering her in return for...for what? Herself, her person and her services.

It seemed so little, and yet she knew, instinctively, that it was not. Marriage could never be that, and even if he entered it without love she felt that Rick would take the contract very seriously...as she would herself. It was for so long; it entailed so much; it stretched ahead into a future which she could not possibly foresee, and which frightened her with its uncertainty.

She shivered in the stiff breeze that cut across these uplands from the high reaches of the Welsh mountains, cool even on a hot June day, and slowly retraced her path. It was not the answer. She couldn't marry him. The prospect was too alarming and the morality of such a step questionable.

As she came around the wing of the house to the front entrance she saw, with a sudden, visceral shock that knotted up her stomach, the cream and brown auctioneer's van drawn up outside. Men in overalls were carting out the furniture she had grown up with...all the old pieces, including those Marissa had determinedly earmarked for herself...the occasional table, her mother's chair, the piano...

Horrified, she rushed indoors, almost colliding with Vicky in the doorway, but she did not stop to brood on her stepmother's self-satisfied expression.

She found her father in his study, and in his eyes as he turned to face her she read a furtive, half-defiant shame. He knew he had betrayed her, and in that moment something between them was broken which would take a long time mending—if, indeed, it were capable of being restored. Marissa felt desperately alone, cast adrift from the familiar moorings of home and family which support and sustain us all. She felt that now she had no one, and nothing, to call her own.

'So you sold it, after all.' she said quietly, tonelessly, incapable of any more anger. 'You didn't let me keep any of it, not even Mother's piano.'

He gestured helplessly.

'I had to. We need the money,' he said. 'And although it's going to the salerooms, that's only a formality. Someone—I have no idea who—has already bought it, from the valuers' specifications, and insisted that it was all or nothing. My hands are tied, Marissa. Try to understand.'

She turned away, wordlessly, not trusting herself to answer, ran upstairs and shut herself in her room. Waves of nausea swept over her as she lay face down on her bed, pain throbbing unbearably at her temples. She felt as weak and helpless as she had the day she was admitted to hospital—all those patient weeks of slow recovery gone for nothing, she thought, assailed by panic and a new, very real fear.

What would she do if she relapsed once more into illness, now or in the future? Soon she would no longer have a home in any true sense of the word. Vicky had made it plain she would be unwelcome with them, and Vicky, anyhow, was the last person she would want around in her hour of need. As for her father—Marissa choked, almost vomited, controlling her body's reactions with difficulty—his 'hands were tied'. She felt as alone and abandoned as an unwanted orphan.

It was a night Marissa would never forget. She didn't sleep, but lay watching the rectangle of her window brighten with the early dawn, as a sense of the awful inescapability of fate took hold of her.

There was only one person who could offer her any sort of refuge, hold out any lasting solution to her present dilemma. Married to Rick, she would never be homeless, and if she were not well, unable to work, there was no doubt she would be taken care of. The demanding ruthlessness in him that she had feared could also be seen as strength...strength which she, at this crisis point in her life, so badly needed. There was, quite simply, no one else to whom she could turn.

'Now then, Miss Marissa, this won't do,' Mrs Reed said reprovingly, bringing her a vast breakfast of bacon, eggs, tomatoes, toast and tea. 'You left your tray outside your door last night, and I swear you never touched a mouthful! It's too thin you are as it is, and look at those dark circles under your eyes!'

Marissa sipped a little of the tea and attempted to bite a slice of toast, but she couldn't face more, and the housekeeper's worried frown deepened.

'I don't know what this house is coming to! Squire looks like thunder this morning—him and Mrs B were having a few words when I took in their tea, and for once she wasn't getting the better of it!'

Marissa raised weary eyebrows, beyond feeling any satisfaction that all was not well in her father's love-nest.

'*I'm* not averse to a bit of gossip, but I should tread very carefully with the new owner when he moves in,' she said drily.

Mrs Reed's face was torn between sympathy and optimism.

'It's a real shame you have to leave here, Miss Marissa—we all feel that way,' she said. 'But don't worry about us. I'm sure that nice Mr Jablonski'll be a pleasure to work for. Thanked us all beautifully, after the dinner, he did, and slipped us all a tenner.'

'Did he now?' Marissa essayed a faint smile. Rick knew how to get people on his side, no doubt about it!

Alone again, she forced herself to finish the toast, then very gingerly got out of bed. The debilitating weakness of last night, brought on by the stress of emotion, had mercifully faded, but she still felt fragile and insecure, and today she certainly must not disgrace herself by fainting.

She dressed very carefully in a soft, fluid dress of fine pale green cotton, and disguised the effects of the near-sleepless night with skilful make-up. Wearing high heels, and definitely not up to walking into the village, she needed transport, but she had no intention of asking her father or Vicky for the loan of a car. She was through asking either of them for anything. They wouldn't listen to her, didn't care about her feelings, so from now on she would go her own way.

It was at the wheel of the old estate Land Rover that Marissa drove into Bishopswell. 'Meet me in the bar of the Black Lion at twelve on Thursday,' had been Rick's last, peremptory command. She parked the disreputable but sturdy vehicle alongside the gleaming convertible which signalled that he was already there, as he had agreed to be.

She could still turn around, drive away, and escape this strange fate that was rushing headlong towards her. Without job, home or family, she could run away and hide somewhere, exist somehow, lick her wounds and suffer, and find a way to survive, she told herself.

But, now she had come this far, a force stronger than any she had ever known was driving her on, urging her to grasp the nettle and accept the challenge. What was there to go back to...half a life, lost, purposeless, adrift.

A matched pair, Rick Jablonski had called them. She prayed he would never know the full measure of the desperation which had sent her running to him this morning. Prayed she was equal to anything he could ask of her, in return for what he was offering.

Squaring her shoulders, forcing a smile to her lips, Marissa marched resolutely through the door, feeling like a Roman gladiator, entering the arena to screaming crowds and certain danger.

'We who are about to die salute you,' she murmured under her breath.

CHAPTER SIX

'SO WHAT you're saying, in effect—although in rather a roundabout way—is that the answer is yes?' said Rick Jablonski amusedly, tapping the fingers of one hand on his glass, but making no move to drink the contents.

Marissa gulped, thinking faintly that she must be mad. Marry *this* man—tie herself to him for life?

'Well, yes but before one signs any contract it's usual to iron out the details first.' she demurred. 'There are things I need to know. For instance, would you expect me to give up modelling completely?'

'I've nothing against working wives in principle, particularly when it's economically necessary,' he said. 'But that would hardly apply to you. And the whole point of this arrangement is for you to be there as and when I need you, not away in the Caribbean, or Thailand, or wherever. Believe me, you'd be too fully occupied to be bored. And I would sometimes expect you to travel with me.'

He paused.

'Apart from the obvious fact that your health requires you to take a long break, I never had the impression that the job was desperately important to you,' he observed. 'At least, not compared to your feelings for Grafton Court, and all this. Am I right?'

'I suppose so,' she admitted reluctantly, a little unnerved by his too shrewd understanding of her. 'You could say I stumbled into it accidentally, and I never expected to be as successful as I have been. I've enjoyed it, yes, but I only left home in the first place to get away from Vicky.'

His smile was slow and assured.

'So I wouldn't exactly be depriving you of anything vital to your well-being,' he said. 'What else is bothering you, Marissa? I'm sure that's not the whole of it.'

If Marissa had possessed the kind of skin which tended to blush, it would have been bright red now. As it was, she avoided his eyes and looked down at the table, thankful that they were in a secluded corner of the lounge bar, with no one else within listening distance.

'There is something else, but I hardly know how to put it,' she began, and Rick interrupted with a short laugh.

'Directly is usually the best way,' he advised. 'You're unlikely to shock or offend me with a sensible question, so shoot from the hip.'

She drew a deep breath, but, much as she would have liked to follow his advice, she found it was not all that easy.

'This... marriage. Is it to be purely a business arrangement? In name only? Or had you planned on our really being man and wife?'

To her annoyance, he laughed again, but this time with real amusement.

'You mean, will we sleep together?' he rephrased her question more frankly. And now it seemed to Marissa that the corner where they sat, and indeed the entire room, was full of him. She was aware of his long legs stretched out in front of him, his shoulders square against the oak settle, the largeness and nearness of his body dominating everything, and she shivered. To share a bed with him, to be possessed and dominated by that body, to have those hands running over her...

But it was not exactly repugnance she felt. Far from it. Excitement, curiosity, a tingling frisson of fear...she did not know which prospect disturbed her most, that of having to sleep with him, or being told she wasn't attractive enough to him to be desired in that way.

She nodded mutely, still unable to look at him.

'Well now,' he said, after making her wait for a tantalising pause, during which he pretended to consider what she was sure he must already have given plenty of thought. 'There doesn't seem to be a whole lot of logic in having a beautiful wife and sleeping alone, does there?'

He shifted his position slightly, and from that angle she could no longer escape the probing gaze that pursued her.

'We're both young and healthy, and you're not sworn to celibacy, are you? It's all right—'as she made a faint sound of protest '—I'm not going to question your past. That's your business, and since you're only twenty-two I've probably got a good deal more to answer for.'

'I don't want to know,' she said quickly, and he smiled.

'That's good, since I wasn't about to tell you. We enter this relationship with a clean slate. Why don't we just let things develop, and take their natural course? There's no desperate hurry, is there?'

Startled tawny eyes looked directly into his blue

ones now. It was not the answer Marissa had expected. Rick had said he thought her beautiful, and somehow she had thought he would be the kind of man to take instant possession of what was lawfully his, to stamp his ownership upon her. Even where love was not involved.

It occurred to her, then, that she knew virtually nothing about him...she did not even have any idea if there was currently a woman in his life. Since he was asking *her* to marry him, she assumed there was no one serious, but he seemed so essentially virile that she was surprised by his unhurried attitude towards sex...at least, where she was concerned. Surely he must feel some desire for her?

And surely she should not be worrying about his lack of impatience! The truth was, he frightened her a little, and she was grateful for the suggestion that they should get to know one another a little better before their relationship moved on to a more intimate plane. He had let her off the hook, and that should be sufficient for her, without her having to question his motives.

'I think you're right. I'm certainly not in a rush,' she said quickly. 'After all, we hardly know one another, do we?'

'We know where we stand. You know what I want, and I know what *you* want out of the deal,' said Rick, rather curtly. 'That's the basis of a good working liaison, in my opinion. And if we've now ironed out all those details in the small print of the contract with which you were so concerned, are we in a position to consider ourselves engaged?'

'I suppose so,' Marissa said slowly.

He grinned.

'Watch this, then.'

Standing up, he waved to Mrs Cooke behind the bar, and called out jubilantly, 'Gill, break open a crate of your best champagne—drinks all round, for everyone here. Marissa and I just decided to get married.'

Amid the cheerful babble of congratulations and surprise that ensued, Marissa sat rooted to her seat until Rick took her hand and gently, but quite insistently, prised her out of it, drawing her to her feet, one arm firmly around her waist.

'What on earth did you do that for?' she whispered furiously. 'The word will fly round Bishopswell faster than Concorde, and we haven't even told my father yet!'

'Of course not—how could we have? I've just this minute proposed to you, and been accepted,' he reminded her, with the ghost of a grin still lingering on his lips. 'Don't worry, we'll drive right over to Grafton Court while this lot are still busy celebrating at my expense.'

His arm still tight around her waist, he handed her a brimming goblet of the bubbling wine Gill Cooke was delightedly passing round.

'Our reasons for this arrangement are our own business, Marissa,' he said quietly in her ear. 'We're not obliged to divulge them to anyone else. So far as the rest of the world is concerned, this is a traditional love-match. So smile, and look into my eyes.'

She was so dumbfounded that she did indeed gaze speechlessly up at him. He bent and kissed her, murmurs of 'Ah...!' echoed round the room, and someone clapped, an activity which was quickly taken up.

'The whole world loves a lover,' Rick said

lightly. Marissa, engulfed in a flood of general
goodwill, stood clasped firmly in the embrace of
this man she hardly knew, said nothing, and knew
herself to be a fraud.

She was greatly relieved when they managed to
escape out into the car park, but knew that her
reprieve was shortlived. For, now the news was out,
she definitely could not renege on her acceptance,
and everyone would very shortly know all about her
supposed whirlwind romance with the fascinating
American.

'Do we have to keep up this pretence throughout
the engagement?' she asked doubtfully. 'Rick, I
agreed to marry you, but I'm not an actress. I can't
guarantee to give the world's best Oscar-winning
performance of a woman in love!'

He shrugged.

'That's up to you. Do you want everyone to say
you're a heartless little gold-digger who's only
after my money?' he challenged. 'Tell you
what—I'll make it easier on you. We'll keep the
engagement short. Tomorrow we'll buy the ring,
see the vicar, all that kind of thing. We can be
married in the middle of July'

Marissa gasped.

'Rick! That's less than a month!'

'Sooner the better,' he said composedly. 'We'll
go away somewhere for a few weeks—how about
the South of France?—and when we come back
Grafton Court will be ready for us to move right in.'

He opened the door of the convertible and helped
her in, still too bemused to object.

'Leave the Land Rover—I'll have it driven over,'
he said easily—not that Marissa had actually given
it a thought. 'We'd better get you home and break

the news before the wires start buzzing with it!'

Davis Beaumont was absolutely delighted to learn that his daughter was going to marry Rick Jablonski. Now he could both have his cake and eat it. The money from the sale of Grafton Court was still his, Vicky got her new house in Cheltenham, and enough ready cash to appease her appetite for the foreseeable future, and his conscience was salved with regard to Marissa. Not only did she get to be mistress of this old place which meant so much to her, but she got a rich husband to boot! It could hardly have worked out better.

Marissa was remarkably quiet and subdued as more champagne was broken out, but he reflected that she was probably stunned by the magnitude of her good fortune. Not that she wasn't a pretty girl, but money usually married money, and she was damned lucky to have netted Rick, all things considered!

'You two certainly haven't wasted any time,' Vicky observed archly, her knowing blue eyes telling Marissa in no uncertain terms that she for one had her own suspicions about this union. 'You Americans don't hang around!'

'When we see a good thing, we tend to grab it,' he agreed, taking Marissa's cold hand in his. Curiously, she found his warm steady grip oddly comforting at this moment, and her fingers curled instinctively around his.

'How sweet!' Vicky said cloyingly. 'When do you plan to have the wedding? September would be nice, I think. The weather is usually settled then, and people are back from their holidays. It would give us a little time to arrange things, wouldn't it,

Davy?'

'We thought the middle of next month,' Rick pressed on unconcernedly, and Vicky's hand flew to her mouth.

'So soon? That's impossible!' she exclaimed. 'Much as I admire your ardour, Rick, you men don't realise—weddings can't be organised in five minutes! There's so much to do.'

Marissa came to life.

'Don't fuss, Vicky. We don't need a big extravaganza,' she said shortly. 'Rick and I can easily get a licence and have a quiet register office wedding.'

She knew she was playing into her stepmother's hands. The last thing Vicky would enjoy was a great drama with another female at the centre of it. But she just wanted this discussion to be over.

'The hell we will, darling,' Rick said amiably, holding her hand even more tightly, squeezing it until the blood ceased to flow to her finger ends. 'Getting married is not a thing you do every day, and I want it done right. The church at Bishopswell—you want to be married here, surely—with you in a white dress and me in a penguin suit. Right? Flowers, cake, music, photographs—the lot. And yes, it *can* all be arranged in time, even in England, if you have enough money and determination. Don't anybody try to tell me it can't!'

'But, Rick——' Marissa began to protest, and got no further.

'Excuse us, folks,' he pulled her to her feet. Without stopping to listen to anything she might have to say, he shepherded her out of the room, down the corridor, and out into the garden.

'Now listen to me,' he said, the amiable tone wiped out and a stern, implacable expression on his face. 'Let's just get this straight. If we're getting married, we're doing it properly, otherwise we can forget the whole thing. I don't want a hole-and-corner business that will leave everyone speculating whether I've got you into trouble. I know a lot of people who will expect to be invited, and there's bound to be a fair amount of media attention too.'

'Another public relations exercise?' she queried, with slight bitterness. 'This year's event, the Jablonski wedding!'

'If you like,' he conceded. 'So if you aren't prepared to see it through in style, for heaven's sake, say so now, and all we'll have is egg on our faces for a few days.'

Marissa knew precisely who would have the eggy face if she backed out now, after Rick had telegraphed their engagement to the entire village.

'I know how to smile for the camera, and I've modelled wedding gowns often enough!' she snapped tersely. Then her anger faded, and she felt her body go limp with sudden exhaustion. 'It's just that I hadn't planned on a big wedding.'

'It's only one day, Marissa,' he told her coolly. 'You owe me that much—and yourself as well. Presumably it will be the only wedding day you'll have.'

She looked at him, troubled by fresh anxieties.

'Rick…what if it doesn't work out…'

'Marriages, like business deals, don't work or not work of their own accord,' he told her decisively. 'They're made to do so by the will and energy of the protagonists, and if they fail it's because said protagonists haven't put a hundred and ten per cent into it. This is a partnership, Marissa. Can you or can you not deliver *your* side?'

And that was a challenge, one that stiffened her nerve and restored her spirits.

'Anything *you* can do, Mr Jablonski,' she said defiantly. 'Come on, let's go back inside before the champagne goes flat!'

She was a little less sure of herself two days later when she picked up a copy of the local newspaper and saw, halfway down the front page, a photograph of herself.

'Love at First Glance'—the headline ran, and went on rapturously:

> American property developer Rick Jablonski, 36, thought he had found the perfect home when he made an offer to buy fifteenth-century Grafton Court, the half-timbered country manor house currently owned by Mr Davis Beaumont.
>
> But he hadn't bargained on being bowled over by Mr Beaumont's ravishing daughter Marissa, 22, a well-known model. Love conquers all, however, and the couple are to marry next month, after a whirlwind courtship. Asked if it was love at first glance, Mr Jablonski would only say, "I know a good thing when I see it."

'Ugh!' Marissa exclaimed, folding up the paper hurriedly, and ramming it into her bag. 'Love at first glance, indeed! I'll kill him when I *do* see him!'

But Rick was dismissively cheerful and nonchalant about the article.

'What's the big deal, Marissa? Everyone enjoys a nice romantic story,' he laughed. 'I thought all women did. Trust me to pick one who's different!'

'But *this* story involves me, and it's not true,' she pointed out acidly. 'I'd like to know where their reporter got hold of all these details.'

'That's easy—from my publicity department,' he told her.

'You mean to say it's all part of your image-building process?' she said disgustedly. 'Rick, when I said I'd marry you, I didn't agree to become part of a three-ring circus!'

'*I* have to get something out of this,' he told her, rather coldly. '*You* have Grafton Court. You also have that, to be going on with.' He glanced at the large diamond cluster on the third finger of her left hand, which had taken her breath away when he had first slid it on.

'Rick, I can't wear anything as expensive as that!' she had protested.'

'Nothing but the best for my wife,' he had grinned laconically, and she soon learned that he meant it quite literally. She not only had *carte blanche*, she was under strict orders to spend extravagantly on her wedding dress and trousseau. No penny-pinching, he had said sternly; it would show, and he wouldn't countenance it. Marissa knew, logically, that it was all part of the role he expected her to play, but none the less she felt very uneasy about spending so much that she still could not think of as hers.

Now she said stiffly, 'I'm not after your money, Rick. It doesn't interest me. I'd have been content just to stay on at Grafton Court, living as I always used to.'

'*I* know that,' he said easily. 'But you can't—not married to me. Your life style has got to change some. There are always sacrifices to be made, Marissa. There's always a price for anything that we want badly enough.'

'I'd like to know what *you're* sacrificing,' she had muttered darkly, and the glance he shot her was wry and cynical.

'You'd be surprised,' was all he would say.

The vicar of Bishopswell, when they called on him, said he would be only too delighted to marry them—after all, he had known Marissa and her father for many years, and it was fitting that she should be married here. But they must appreciate that he couldn't possibly fit them in on a Saturday, Saturdays being booked solidly for months ahead. In fact, he didn't have one free until well into October.

'It has to be July,' Rick insisted, politely but quite firmly. 'It doesn't matter what day of the week. How about the fifteenth? That's a Friday.'

And so the church was booked. Marissa gasped when she saw the list of invitations to be sent out.

'Rick, who *are* all these people?'

'Oh—friends, business acquaintances, family. Get on the phone to Hereford, Marissa, and block-book as much hotel accommodation as you can. We'll probably need it,' he said calmly. 'How about bridesmaids? You've no young female relatives you have to oblige, have you?'

'No,' she said, a little breathless at the speed and scope of his organisation. 'But there's my flatmate and another friend from London.'

'Good. I have two young nieces. We'll have to rope them in,' he said, scribbling swiftly on the notepad in front of him. 'And there's my brother—he'll have to be best man.'

'I didn't even know you *had* a brother,' she said faintly.

'Yes. Jan—Janusz—he works for me too,' he told her. 'You'll like him, I know. And even though our parents are dead, there's a whole host of Polish relatives in America who'll have to come over. I suggest a marquee in the grounds of Grafton Court for the reception, but I'll leave you to organise all that side of it.'

And so she did, drowning in a tidal wave of smoked salmon and Veuve Clicquot, feeling progressively, as the days passed, that this was not a wedding she was planning—certainly not *her* wedding day…but a kind of grand opera. It was just as well, she told herself soberly, that she was not approaching it with romantic notions, because, if she had been, all this would undoubtedly have knocked them out of her!

A week before the wedding, Rick took off for Europe, telling her only that he might well not be back before the fourteenth, but that he was sure she was capable of finalising all the arrangements without his assistance.

Marissa had few doubts about that, for all she knew that he would sure as hell expect everything to be perfect. What did trouble her was his prolonged absence in the final run-up to the wedding, and she found, much to her own surprise, that she resented his disappearance, and would have preferred to see as much of him as possible during those last few days immediately prior to becoming Mrs Jablonski.

It would be like walking down the aisle with a stranger, she thought, and shouldn't couples on the verge of marriage *want* to be together? Not if it were little more than a business deal, she reminded herself—why should Rick put off legitimate business for a woman he didn't love, who would be readily available in a few days' time?

So why was she feeling so lost and in need of his presence?

'Got the pre-wedding jitters, then?' laughed Gill Cooke, when Marissa bumped into her in the village. 'I can tell from your face. We all get that sudden, awful feeling that this is the last thing we want to do, however much in love we are. It'll all come right when you wake up on The Day.'

Marissa could only smile guiltily in reply, and was further cast down when Rick phoned her that night from Amsterdam to say no way could he get back before the fourteenth.

'I want this all wrapped up, so I can take time off without worrying about it,' he said, reasonably enough. Her silence must have told him something, and he added, half jokingly, 'Missing me, are you?'

'Don't be silly!' she denied hotly, at once. 'It's just that I seem to have been left to do everything at this end.'

'I thought women enjoyed that kind of thing,' Rick said airily. And then the timbre of his voice changed, became rougher, deeper, as he said, 'I'll make up for my absence, don't worry.'

Marissa hung up, shaking uncontrollably with an emotion she could not name. He was several hundred miles away, the connection broken, but she could still hear the potent promise implicit in his voice.

Turning, she met her stepmother's shrewd, percipient blue eyes, agleam with vicarious excitement.

'Lover-boy, was it?' Vicky enquired lightly. 'Or is that the wrong description? Because, of course, you aren't in love with him, are you?'

'I don't know why you say that,' Marissa challenged. Vicky was the last person to whom she would be likely to make such an admission. 'He's extremely attractive—you said so yourself—and oozes charisma. I'm never bored in his company.' This, at least, she could say in all honesty.

'And he's stinking rich, which can't hurt!' Vicky laughed maliciously. 'Clever girl! At a stroke, you get Grafton Court *and* a wealthy husband. As they say on all the sports programmes, you've played a blinder!'

Marissa turned away, but her stepmother had not finished.

'There'll be a reckoning, you know,' she said softly. 'You'll have to pay for what you're getting. And with a man like Rick I'd imagine the payments would have to be made in bed. Well, that could be fun, but only if you're woman enough.'

Her laughter echoed behind her as she left the room, and Marissa was seized by a chill apprehension. He'd said he wouldn't hurry her, and since their engagement the most contact they had shared had been a brief squeeze of the hand, a perfunctory kiss on her cheek. But, admittedly, she had seen very little of him. That would change when they were married. They would be together all the time on honeymoon. How long would he be satisfied with that state of affairs?

She knew she was both afraid of and attracted by his intense masculinity, and Vicky's taunt had disturbed her afresh. Her only previous affair, several years ago, had been brief, hurtful and unsatisfactory. It had not awakened her, and she had no idea of how to keep a man happy in bed. A man like Rick, who, for all his reticence on the subject, must have had plenty of experience with women.

She was tense and worried for what remained of the week, and on the eve of the wedding, when Rick phoned her from the Black Lion to say he was safely back, she was suddenly desperately eager to see him, to look into his eyes and reassure herself that it would be all right. That he was not some rapacious satyr, but Rick—a man, a human being, who could be thoughtful and considerate and sensitive.

'I'm glad you made it,' she said, forcing a light laugh. 'Would you like to come over for a drink?'

'Marissa, it's supposed to be bad luck for the groom to see the bride the night before the wedding,' he reminded her. 'We'll not court disaster.'

'But, Rick, that's terribly old-fashioned!' she had protested, dismayed.

He laughed, but was adamant.

'I *am* old-fashioned, honey. Didn't you know? I know I'm irresistible, but try to contain your impatience for a few more hours.'

The mildly sarcastic chuckle in his voice enraged her, and she all but slammed the receiver down. Then he said softly, 'See you in church, firebrand,' and hung up himself. And there was nothing for it but to endure alone her torment of nervous anticipation.

The morning of the fifteenth dawned fresh and bright. There had been a sprinkling of rain during the night, leaving the lawns and the field beyond damply sparkling. Marissa gazed out at the huge marquee in the south field, where the linen-draped tables would later be laden with the expensive buffet she had arranged, and silver buckets cooling the champagne. She drew a deep breath. This was her wedding day, and her pulse beat swiftly with excitement at the thought of it, in spite of everything.

Eating the traditional breakfast in bed brought to her by a smiling Mrs Reed, she tried to envisage Rick, in the dining-room of the Black Lion, with the brother she had not even met. She quailed at the thought of all those unknown Polish-American friends and relatives, fearful in case they didn't like her.

Very soon it was time to get ready, with the help of her bridesmaids, Suzanne, the friend with whom she had first stayed when she left home and went to live in London, and Bunty, who had shared her flat.

'This is just like a film!' Suzanne sighed enviously, drooling as she helped Marissa into her dress. 'But then your whole life has been like that, hasn't it, Marissa? Growing up in this place—the ancestral home, and all that. Then being discovered, and whisked away to a glamorous job, travelling the world, your face over all the glossy mags. Now, finally, meeting a terrific man, with pots of money. Some girls have all the luck!'

Marissa looked wryly at her reflection in the mirror. Did they, indeed? Certainly, she scarcely recognised this dreamlike creature in the ivory satin and lace confection, moulded to the hip, from where the skirt belled out gently, the neckline high and demure at the front, but low at the back, the view of her that most people would see in church. The stiffened petticoats—one of them blue—rustled beneath her skirts as she turned to ensure that the veil was pinned firmly to the pearl-encrusted head dress over her dark, shining, upswept hair. What would Rick think? Would he approve of this picture? Would she live up to the image she wondered, swallowing a sudden sour taste in her mouth.

Vicky, in brilliant royal blue, an outrageous little feathery hat perched on her neatly coiffed blonde curls, popped her head round the door.

'The little bridesmaids are here,' she announced sharply. 'I have to go now—the cars have come.'

Marissa scarcely had time to glance at the fleet of limousines cruising slowly up the drive, before the two small girls in their peach and white dresses were virtually pushed at her. Gown rustling, she dropped to her knees to approach them closer to their level.

'Hi,' she said. 'I'm Marissa, and I'm scared. Are you scared too?'

They giggled, the elder one displaying silver braces across her teeth, and Marissa was suddenly touched. In his exacting desire to have this wedding stage-managed and perfect to the minutest detail, Rick had not stooped to hurting this little girl's feelings by excluding her. Braces and all, she was going to be a bridesmaid. Something about this reassured Marissa, buoying up her own confidence so that she went out to join her father with a smile on her face.

Today, at least, his joy and the tears springing to his eyes were genuine.

'You're beautiful, *cariad*,' he whispered. 'As lovely a bride as this old house has ever seen in all its years.'

'You look pretty smart yourself,' she said,

admiring the dove-grey tails that all the men involved, groom included, would be wearing.

He gave her his arm.

'Time to go,' he said. 'I thank God I'm giving you to a good man. He'll be better for you than I've been.'

Marissa could not bear the bleakness in his voice.

'Oh, come on!' she said lightly. 'None of that nonsense! It's my wedding day.'

And it seemed half the county had turned out to see it. The village was jammed with cars, the churchyard with interested bystanders, and the church itself was packed. There were local people Marissa had known all her life, friends she had made at school and in her work, and there was the big American contingent, all strangers to her, and all smiling as the organist played the Bach fugue she had chosen, and she began her long walk up the aisle.

Her throat was tight with emotion as she walked, as all those other Beaumont brides had done, towards her waiting bridegroom in this ancient church. The echo of their thoughts, their fears, their memories seemed to live on and whisper all around her, supporting and upholding this latest of their long line as she moved through the watchful, admiring congregation of guests and well-wishers. Many of those brides had been given in marriage to men they scarcely knew, and had had to learn to love. She, at least, had made her own choice.

And here he was, turning towards her as she approaches, his tall, broad figure magnificent in the formal dress, the elegance of his attire, his immaculate grooming only emphasising that untamed quality which lay close beneath the veneer.

Beside him, Marissa had a swift impression of a younger, not quite so tall version of Rick, positively beaming at her, radiating the goodwill he could not yet express in words. She smiled back briefly, then all her attention was claimed, seized, by the man about to become her husband. His hand touched hers, his eyes smiled quizzically down at her, and a little light of amusement danced in their sea-green depths.

'So you came, firebrand,' he murmured, half under his breath. 'There's no going back now!'

CHAPTER SEVEN

IF ANYONE had told Marissa, during that long, doubt-plagued week leading up to it, that she would actually enjoy her wedding day, she would probably have laughed in their face.

But something odd had happened to her the minute the vicar took her hands and Rick's and joined them. A surge of confidence and determination flowed through her, and she thought, *yes*, I can. I can do this. I will make him whatever kind of wife he wants, and succeed, and I will live out my life here, as I'd always planned to. Maybe it isn't love, but it will suffice.

She felt herself to be strong, but knew that Rick was stronger, and that, so long as she did not fail or cheat or short-change him in any way, that strength would always be on her side. With it, she could take on the world.

The church doors stood open, and as the familiar strains of the Wedding March flooded into the sunlit churchyard, Marissa, her veil thrown back, emerged on the arm of her new husband, to gasps of pleasure and admiration from those waiting outside. Flashbulbs popped, and she saw, as he had intimated, that the Press had turned out in force to cover this wedding—a romance of the twentieth century par excellence: successful business magnate marries beautiful model.

The final touch—a lovingly restored old open

carriage, drawn by two splendid grey horses, stood waiting at the lych-gate to conduct the newlyweds back to Grafton Court.

'Ye gods!' muttered Rick as they braved the deluge of confetti. 'Was this your idea?'

'Naturally,' she murmured with a smile. 'Anyone can leave church in a limo, Rick—they're ten a penny. Don't you want to make the glossies?'

He grinned.

'You've sure got style, Marissa. But then that's why I married you,' he said, helping her up into the carriage, and just for the briefest of moments, a faint cloud marred the brightness of her day.

The first person waiting to greet her when they arrived at the lavish reception was Rick's brother Jan, who enveloped her in a crushing, unceremonious hug.

'Welcome to the family, little sister!' he said warmly. Not quite so tall as his brother, he could still look down on Marissa. 'If Rick couldn't find himself a nice Polish girl, I swear he did the next best thing! I only wish our parents were alive to see this day. We'd all given up hope of ever marrying him off!'

She had expected to be in awe of the large, vociferous Polish-American crowd of relatives, cousins, aunts, and uncles who had flown the Atlantic especially for the wedding, but if anything she was overwhelmed by the warmth and generosity of their welcome. Quite simply, they took her to them, accepted her as one of their number, and she was heartened by this genuine, spontaneous affection which reached out to draw her in—even if they did lapse into Polish with alarming frequency, so that she hadn't a clue what was being said to or about her. No matter—the goodwill was palpable.

'Gracious!' Vicky said caustically, 'what *have* you let yourself in for, Marissa? Just listen to them all, babbling away in that diabolical language that sounds like broken glass! Why can't they speak English?'

Unexpectedly, Rick appeared behind them, his hand resting on Marissa's shoulder.

'They can, of course, and they do, most of the time,' he said. His voice was urbane and calm, but she knew him well enough to sense the veiled anger. 'But the roots are deep, and in times of strong emotion one reverts.'

He drew her away, turning his back on Vicky, and leaving her with mouth agape. Marissa saw, with some relief, that his anger was not targeted on her.

'Actually, I think it isn't at all like breaking glass. It sounds rather musical, like Welsh, which is almost as unintelligible to most English speakers.' She smiled. 'Would you like me to learn Polish?'

Rick looked surprised by the offer.

'You could always try. It's not strictly necessary, but it would be a nice gesture to pick up a smattering,' he said. 'I'll teach you myself, if you'd like.'

'I wasn't thinking of it as a gesture,' she said drily. 'It occurred to me that whenever your family visit, I won't have the faintest idea what's going on!'

After that, it all had the hazy, fuzzy-edged quality of a dream in her memories. His hand over hers on the knife cutting the cake. More photographs, champagne and speeches. Her father, once again looking as if he might burst into tears at any moment. More photos, more champagne. And the singing—the Poles, like the Welsh, had a tendency to burst spontaneously into lusty, melodious song, and the sound of the deep-throated, rhythmic harmony, in a language she could not understand, followed Marissa as she went up to her room to change.

Her room? But was it actually hers any longer? When she returned, would things have changed irrevocably? Would she be sharing the master bedroom with Rick, the bedroom the master and mistress of Grafton Court had always used, for four centuries? Marissa shivered as Suzanne and Bunty helped her out of the layers of lace and silk and frothy petticoats.

'Goose walked over your grave?' jested Bunty. 'Poor thing, you're only off to the South of France with your gorgeous, rich, absolutely super husband! Want to swap places and go back to the flat instead of me?'

Marissa only smiled as she slipped into the straight-skirted little suit in lemon and green springtime print, and adjusted the wide-brimmed picture hat on her dark hair. Would she turn away from this chosen destiny, if she were miraculously offered the chance? She honestly could not say.

But you can't, she told herself soberly. This is real, not a rehearsal...you've done it, you're married. She sought desperately for a resurgence of that confidence which had strengthened her as she stood at the altar earlier, and which had carried her through the day. Easy, easy, surrounded by all these laughing, singing, well-wishing people, but very soon they would be alone, just Rick and herself, and where was that courage now?

Suzanne handed her her slim white leather clutch-bag.

'There you go. Don't do anything *I* wouldn't enjoy,' she grinned.

Cold, scared, and suddenly deflated, Marissa went slowly down the stairs towards her husband and her future—a bride going on her honeymoon, as fearful as a condemned victim en route to the executioner's block.

They drove off in the red convertible, crossed the Channel, and boarded the motorail to Avignon.

'I suppose we could have flown,' said Rick, 'but I've grown attached to this car—I want it at the other end. Besides, it's pleasant to go to sleep in the darkness, half-way across France, and to wake up next morning in the South!'

He had reserved a first-class sleeper compartment for them, and they ate in the dining car as the train sped on its way, the summer dusk falling beyond the moving picture of the lighted windows. Then, tactfully, he allowed her to retire first—like a bridegroom in a Victorian novel, she thought—while he finished his coffee and brandy.

Marissa took off her clothes with numb, nerveless fingers, fumbling with the buttons and catches, trying to hurry, since she did not want to be in a half-undressed state when Rick made an appearance. She did not know what to expect of this, their first night together. 'We'll let things take their natural course,' he had said, but what was more natural than for a man to make love to his wife on their wedding night.

Her first and only experience had been years ago,

when she had been a naïve young model, bowled over by a predatory photographer. He'd treated her roughly, with little consideration for her feelings, and she'd blotted out the memory as time passed. Only now it came back to haunt her.

She put on her écru satin nightdress, slipped her arms into the matching négligé, and sat shivering, perched uneasily on the edge of the bunk. Surely she did not expect Rick to behave with the same careless ignorance as her first lover? On the occasions when he had touched her, she recalled how pleasurable she had found it—even that episode in his car had filled her with a savage excitement. Was that why she was so keyed up, as if she were about to explode with suppressed anticipation? Fear or desire—Marissa did not truly know which of these two fierce emotions predominated.

She must have presented a woebegone picture of a blushing bride, for when Rick came in a short while later he paused for a moment, looked at the girl hunched on the bunk, shrugged, smiled, and disappeared into their private washroom. He emerged, clad in navy silk pyjamas, and glanced with amusement at the champagne cooling in its ice-bucket.

'Did I order that final seductive detail? I suppose I must have done,' he grinned. 'I don't know about you, but I've had quite enough of that stuff for one day. Shall we give it a miss?'

Reaching out to adjust the blind at the window more securely, he accidentally brushed her shoulder, and Marissa jumped like a scalded cat. His expression, as he regarded her, resembled that of a coach whose pupil dared not risk the high dive.

'There's no need to look at me like that. If I were inclined to pounce on you and have my wicked way, these couchettes aren't ideally suited for the purpose,' he drawled. 'Tell you what—why don't we get some sleep? It's been a long day for both of us.'

She nodded mutely, so overcome with relief that she could have kissed him out of sheer gratitude. Perversely, she had a strong need to hold him, to feel the security of those firm arms around her. But she couldn't have it both ways, seeking comfort from him and giving nothing in return.

Marissa lay in her bunk in the darkness as the train swayed south. She had no way of knowing if her new husband was actually sleeping, for all his breathing sounded relaxed and even. She knew it was going to be very difficult for her to sleep at all, conscious as she was of him, lying only a few feet away from her.

Would it have been better if he had indeed ignored or overridden her nervousness and exhaustion, stripped her naked and taken her, regardless? Until he did, until she was over that hurdle, she knew she was doomed to be a tangled skein of nerves and responses.

Marissa turned on her side, pounded the pillow with her fist, and eventually allowed the motion of the train to lull her into an uneasy sleep, in place of the lover she did not have.

From the gracious Papal city of Avignon they drove south-east through the sun-bleached, rosemary-scented hills of Provence. Marissa recalled this part of France from a working trip, when, despite a tight schedule leaving little personal time, she had savoured briefly the breathtaking beauty and the very special atmosphere.

'You can well understand,' said Rick, pulling up to look out over the stunning vista of Cap Ferrat, with its green pines hiding the while villas set among them, and the shimmering azure sea beyond, 'why people who can afford to live anywhere in the world choose to settle here.'

He glanced obliquely at Marissa, her eyes veiled by tinted glasses.

'A more romantic location than this for a honeymoon is difficult to imagine,' he added.

Her heart began to pound nervously again.

'But we aren't romantic. This honeymoon, like the wedding, and the engagement, is simply part of a charade put on for the Press and public,' she said.

'Slightly different, I'd say. The Press and public haven't come along with us,' he replied softly, in a voice that whispered along her nerves, causing her to stiffen with anxiety.

All the same, she had to gasp when she saw the villa where they were to stay, hugging the hillside high above a tiny village. A vine-shaded terrace at ground level, and a balcony above, looked out over an inviting swimming-pool, terraced gardens bright with flowers and scented shrubs, and, far below, the clear turquoise of the Mediterranean.

Rick swung the car to a smooth halt outside, and a politely smiling manservant emerged to open the doors and take their luggage from the car boot, while a matronly woman in a black dress stood at the doorway to welcome them. Inside, the floors were all Provençal patterned tiles; the furnishings bespoke a simple, understated luxury, cool and perfectly suited to the hot, sunny climate.

The manservant carried their luggage upstairs and they followed him. Marissa eyed up the sleeping arrangements swiftly. The main bedroom, to which he had automatically conducted them, was interconnected, via a vast marble bathroom, to a further bedroom beyond.

She smiled at the manservant and addressed him in the efficient French she had learned at boarding school, asking him if he would please take her case into the other bedroom. After a moment's politely veiled surprise, he concurred, and Marissa followed him, quickly engaging him in conversation she knew Rick could not follow. Using him shamefully as a shield between herself and her husband.

When he finally withdrew, she turned to find Rick behind her. The balcony ran the full length of the first floor, and he had simply strolled out through the open French doors of the main bedroom. Now he stood leaning against the jamb of hers, regarding her quizzically.

'His name is Philippe, his wife is Marie-Laure, and I told him we'll shower and have lunch right away,' she told him, talking, she knew, just a little too rapidly.

'Did you also tell him about the rather weird honeymoon customs we Anglo-Americans have?' he asked, with a sardonic grin.

Marissa bit her lip.

'Rick, you said we wouldn't rush things——' she began.

'I said we'd let nature take its course,' he replied. 'Seems to me we're putting one hell of an obstacle in its path. However, if you want separate bedrooms, you only have to say so—to me. There's no need to resort to obscure stratagems like the one you just pulled.'

She was sufficiently ashamed of herself to look down at the terracotta-tiled floor.

'You've given *me* the best room,' he observed, more gently. 'I'll change with you, if you like.'

'No—this one's fine,' she insisted. It had its own en suite shower-room, so they need not even meet by chance in the palatial bathroom, she noted. 'If you don't mind, I'd like to clean up before lunch.'

He merely shrugged, turned, and retired to his own quarters. If he was annoyed, he did not show it, and appeared perfectly cheerful when Marissa joined him for lunch on the sunny terrace.

'Rick, who does this villa belong to?' she asked, toying with the perfectly composed salade Niçoise on her plate.

'It's mine, of course,' he said placidly, as if the question were unnecessary and the answer self-evident. 'I bought it when I was over here some weeks ago.'

Before she had arranged that fateful dinner party, *before* he had asked her to marry him. Marissa had a vague, uncomfortable feeling that she was part of some long-laid scheme, that, far from being the impulse of one inspired day, the marriage fitted into a plan, a schedule, which suited his future arrangements. Would any suitable woman have served his purpose? Had she simply happened to be in the right place at the right time?

'I reckoned I would need a summer place in Europe, and this seemed as good as anywhere,' he said easily, breaking into her thoughtful silence. 'What's the matter, Marissa? Didn't you think I was rich enough to own property on the Riviera? I assure you I am.'

'Rick, I don't *care* how rich you are,' she told him, and he gave her a long, slow considering look.

'I believe you,' he said. 'There's not an awful lot you *do* care about, outside of that ancestral pile of yours, is there?'

She had meant to indicate that she wasn't after his money, but he had turned her words neatly against her. Glaring at him, she said coldly, 'That's right—just like you with your business empire, and your all-important image!'

He cast her a look of pure disgust. 'I'm going to change and swim in the pool,' he declared. 'Might as well get brown and go home *looking* as if I've had a great time.'

The air between them was cool for most of the afternoon, but swimming and relaxing in the sun could not help but improve their mood.

'What the hell?' grinned Rick, as the sun began to dip behind the hills. 'Go dress up—let's go out to dinner.'

Marissa was only too ready to comply. She put on a white, full-skirted dress and high-heeled sandals, and they drove down through the hills, past crumbling golden-stone villages, stopping to sip a drink at a harbourside restaurant where tall, pastel-washed houses reflected themselves among the fishing fleet.

Finally they ate at an intimate little restaurant in Ste Maxime, gazing across the bay at the winking lights of St Tropez. Rick was charming and amusing, making her laugh with funny stories about their fellow diners.

'That one has to be a murderer. He's probably hidden his wife's body in a wine barrel in the cellar, and shot her lover. The guy in the corner on his own, he's wanted by Interpol for corporate fraud—why d'you reckon he keeps looking over his shoulder?'

Marissa dabbed her eyes, trying not to smudge her mascara.

'How about the ritzy lady over there, with the good-looking young man? A famous actress with her toy boy?'

'You're getting the hang of it,' he said, pouring more wine.

They were still laughing as they walked the steep, cobbled streets in the warm night air, back to where they had parked the car near the elegant marina.

'How about a final cognac on the balcony?' Rick suggested as they arrived back at the villa.

'Lovely,' she agreed, and they sat at the small table outside their bedrooms, looking out over the dark hills with lights sparkling like jewels here and there. Marissa, mellowed by the wine she had drunk, and by his light-hearted manner, was more relaxed than she had been for some time.

'Time to turn in?' he said, draining the glass.

'I suppose so,' she replied, oddly regretful. 'Goodnight, Rick—and thank you for a lovely evening!'

He stood up as she did, catching her by the shoulders.

'That's a little formal, isn't it?' he queried. 'This is more what I had in mind.'

He kissed her very firmly, holding her so tightly she could not move, one hand pressed into the small of her back, the other cupping her chin. She felt herself descending into a vortex, the world spinning with her, and she was unable to breathe or think, eager and afraid at the same time. Her mouth quested for his, seeking more, and he relinquished his grip in order to unzip her dress with swift expertise, easing it over her shoulders, his lips finding her throat.

She gasped and backed away from him.

'Rick—no! You said you'd give me time!' she almost choked, threatened by the sudden onslaught of her own desire, and the speed with which things had got out of hand. She couldn't cope with so much, so soon, the pushing back of frontiers she did not feel ready to cross.

He stood back, motionless, watching as she quickly adjusted her dress.

'How much time are you likely to want, Marissa—or do you even know the answer to that?' he asked levelly. 'It seemed to me that the moment was right—that you wanted it to happen as much as I did. Are you telling me I was wrong?'

'You mean you thought you'd got me nicely softened up with all those funny jokes and plenty of wine, and I'd be an easy push-over?' she replied accusingly. 'So that's what it was all about! And I thought we were having fun, getting to know one another.'

'I sure am trying, lady,' he said laconically. 'But you don't make it easy. OK——' he held up a hand as she opened her mouth to protest, 'I'll back off. Marie-Laure will have one big surprise when she brings the morning coffee! But I wish I knew exactly what it is you're so afraid of!'

With that, he turned and left her, and moments later she heard the shower running in his bathroom.

I wish I knew too, she thought wretchedly, lying alone in the warm navy blue night, listening to the monotonous hum of the cicadas outside. Was it of him—a fear induced by an unhappy past experience—or of herself, a fear of failure, of not being the woman he expected his wife to be? Perfect in this department, as in all others!

In the morning, she found him already on the terrace eating breakfast when she got up. He only smiled and wished her good morning, quite cheerfully, with no reference to yesterday's episode, but Marissa did not feel able to let it pass without saying something.

'Rick—about last night——' she began uneasily.

'Drop it, Marissa.' He bit into a croissant and helped himself to more of the fragrant, steaming coffee. 'I came on too strong, and you weren't willing. What more is there to say?'

She sat down, looking intently into his unrevealing face.

'You may think that way, but I have to say something. I know we don't…we aren't in love with each other, but…if we could become friends before trying to become lovers…am I making any sense?'

There was a long pause before he said, 'The trouble is, can you build a relationship like that, artificially, step by step? These things occur simultaneously. A couple argue, fight, tease one another, make love—it's part of the process of discovering one another, and I don't know if you can separate the strands.' He shrugged. 'But if that's really the way you want it, we can try.'

They tried. For the next few days Rick punctiliously kept his distance from her by day, and made no attempt to invade her bedroom at night. They chatted, smiled, were almost painfully polite and considerate, but, far from getting to know one another, Marissa had to admit they seemed further apart than they had been before their marriage.

They had learned more about one another in the cut and thrust of their encounters shortly after they first met; their conversations then had been spiced with conflict and mutual curiosity. Now their relationship was careful, courteous, and incredibly superficial.

There was unmistakable relief in Rick's voice, one evening, as he said, 'I'm afraid I shall have to desert you for the day tomorrow. I think I warned you there'd be some work involved in this visit.'

He needn't sound quite so happy at the prospect of getting away from her! she thought, with perverse annoyance. It was her inability to understand why she resented his going, when she had spent the best part of a week avoiding intimacy with him, which caused her to snap, 'Surely you're not planning to churn up a few acres of this real estate?'

'I *don't* do that sort of thing, really, as you very well know,' he replied, with some irritation. 'There's a waterpark complex the other side of Marseilles that I'm interested in. Reports suggest it could be a real money-spinner, with a bit of upgrading.'

He looked at her thoughtfully, and she hoped he was going to suggest she accompanied him. Then he said, 'There's no point, really, in your coming along. I'll be involved in discussions for most of the day, and I guess you could get bored with the water chute.'

He was gone in the morning before Marie-Laure brought her coffee. Marissa dressed, breakfasted, and wondered what to do next. The villa was lonely without Rick—the sound of his voice, his large, suntanned body splashing in the pool. She missed the energetic electricity of his presence, and it troubled her that she felt such a lack.

She walked into the village, wandered idly round the outdoor market where stalls full of shiny-skinned aubergines, tomatoes and peppers jostled for place with others selling bikinis and plastic flip-flops. Tiring of this, she ate lunch on a restaurant terrace, but it wasn't any fun eating alone, so, finishing hurriedly, she went for a long walk among the fragrant, quiet, empty reaches of the hills above the village.

Rick had said he would not be home for dinner, and after a long day out in the sun Marissa wanted only a light supper which she ate by the pool before retiring early to bed. Alone—but then she always slept alone. Why then did she feel so strongly the absence of Rick, the knowledge of his being there, unseen, in the adjoining bedroom?

She finally fell asleep, only to be awakened a short while later by the sound of the shower running in the marble bathroom. He was back! Marissa sat bolt upright, startled by the sudden, violent bearing of her own heart, the leap of unexpected gladness. She did not order her feet to propel her out of bed and through the open French doors on to the balcony, but somehow she found herself there, standing in her thin, silky nightdress, the faint breeze lifting her hair slightly from her shoulders.

His doors were open too, and there he was, clad only in pyjama trousers, the powerful muscles of his shoulders and torso emphasised by the faint glow of his bedside lamp.

She heard him catch his breath sharply, but, not realising that the bright moonlight rendered her already revealing nightdress virtually transparent, she could only find banal, obvious words to say.

'You're back.'

'Did you think I wouldn't be?' His eyebrows rose, but his tone was distant, and a swell of angry emotion began to rise within her.

'Who knows? You were certainly glad enough to get away.' she accused, the impetus of her feelings propelling her the final few steps into his room, where she had been careful not to venture before.

'Are you surprised? I can only take so much of this fencing around one another that we've been indulging in,' he said curtly. 'And while I'm very honoured by this midnight visit, I should remind you that you're in my bedroom, Marissa, way out of your territory. I suggest you scurry back to your shell. Aren't you afraid I might pounce on you again?'

The hostile sarcasm of his tone brought sudden tears to her eyes, and she gazed at him through their mist, the lovely features both wounded and bewildered. All desire to argue with him had left her, and she said lamely, 'Rick, I'm sorry. We made a bargain and I've not kept my side of it. I've failed you—already.'

'Hey!' The anger faded from his eyes as he crossed the room, put an arm round her shoulders, and drew her to him. 'Look—don't cry, for goodness' sake! I'm the one who should be sorry. I promised you time, and I meant it, but dammit, I'm only a man, and you're just too unfairly desirable!'

Her tears dampened the already shower-tangled hairs of his chest, and she looked up at him, tawny eyes wide.

'Am I?' she asked hoarsely.

The circle of his arms still enfolded her.

'You must know it!' he exclaimed with a ragged laugh. 'Isn't this the face that launched a thousand *Vogues*, and the body that goes with it?'

'That's not quite the same as being desirable...to you.' Her voice was little more than a whisper.

'I thought I made that more than clear—and that you didn't much care for it,' he said. 'Did you think I wanted to make love to you just because you're here, because you're a woman, who happens to be my wife? I wanted—*want*—*you*, Marissa.'

Deep inside her, a dark, basic excitement stretched and uncurled. The sound of his voice, the moonlight in the room, the touch of his hands on her bare shoulders awoke a strong, sensual re-ponse, transforming her fears into a restless urgency. She ran her hands experimentally up his chest, exploring the hardness of his ribs and the siken elasticity of his muscles. How good he felt!

With a low groan he slid the straps of her nightdress over her shoulders, letting it fall to the ground in a weightless slither, exposing the slim waist, long, slender legs, and the smooth fullness of her breasts to his gaze. She shook back the dark mass of her hair and stood motionless, shivering slightly with fierce anticipation, knowing that her fate was here and now, and there was no escaping it.

His large, strong, capable hands covered her breasts, sending ripples of unbearable pleasure through her, and his mouth crushed down on hers. She had never known there could be sensation such as this, and vaguely, intuitively, she knew it was only the beginning. Fear returned, briefly, as he lifted her on to the bed, and he silenced it firmly with the warmth and strength of his body. And then there was only pure, unalloyed pleasure, which swept her along on its riptide, oblivious and uncaring.

Now, truly, she thought, as she drifted into a brief loss of consciousness, there was no road back.

CHAPTER EIGHT

RICK and Marissa did not emerge from the bedroom until almost lunchtime next day, and being French, and understanding such things, Marie-Laure did not disturb them after her arrival with early morning coffee elicited only a minimal response.

Marissa had gone to his bed last night, not a virgin, it was true, but sexually uneducated in all but a technical sense. By morning she felt as if she possessed a thousand years of deliciously sinful experience. There was not an inch of her he had not explored and awakened, not a sensation undiscovered...or so she thought, until the next time they made love, when she found, to her astonishment, that there was more. Could this go on forever?

'I knew, really, that under all that seemingly frigid restraint was a deeply sensual woman,' he said. 'She just needed persuading out of that shell.'

It was three o'clock, and after a leisured lunch they had retired for a siesta—both of them well aware that this was a mere euphemism for what was really going to happen in the bedroom. The blinds were drawn, and outside, the dead, still hand of the Midi afternoon pressed down heavily, muffling everything under a blanket of heat.

Marissa lay back against a pile of pillows. She was naked, and didn't care; for one thing, it was hot, for another, the pleasure of being looked at by Rick was second only to that of being touched. For the first time her own beauty had acquired a personal meaning and purpose, aside from being merely a tool of her trade.

She said, 'I should have told you I wasn't a virgin. I had…an unhappy experience when I was younger. Someone took me for the silly idiot I must have been, and hurt me badly. It wasn't even good, either—not like this.'

'I'm supposed to be vastly relieved it wasn't an ecstatic happening?' Rick asked, with the suggestion of a smile. 'There's no reason you had to tell me that, Marissa. Your past is your own business.'

'Does that mean I'm not allowed to ask any questions about yours?' she probed, unable to deny that she *was* curious.

'I certainly don't plan on giving you a résumé of my sex life to date,' he declared. 'There's little to be gained by that kind of confidence.'

Except, Marissa thought, mildly rebuffed, it was natural to wish to know more about someone with whom one had indulged in such abandoned intimacies.

'I wouldn't want all the gory details,' she demurred. 'But, Rick, you're thirty-six. Surely you've been in love—at least once?'

He was quiet for a while, then he said, 'There was someone, quite a few years ago, whom I wanted to marry.'

'And?' She sat up, interested.

'And nothing. She had a flourishing career of her own, and I wasn't successful enough for her to consider combining it with marriage to a questionable commodity like myself. We parted friends.'

'You're successful now,' she pointed out.

Rick laughed shortly.

'What are you asking? If I'm turned down once, I don't give second chances. Let it go now, Marissa. The subject is closed. And I'm married to you now, aren't I?'

She laughed and wound her arms round his neck, but for once he hesitated.

'Sometimes I wonder if you weren't right—if I haven't pushed things along too quickly,' he said thoughtfully. 'Perhaps you weren't ready for this—not really.'

'That's crazy! How can you say such a thing?' she demanded. 'What else do I have to do to prove it?'

'You've certainly demonstrated that you enjoy making love,' he admitted. 'But life is not all honeymoon, and this will soon be over; then it will be back to reality. Unless a woman is really mature, and can handle it, sleeping with her tends to make her possessive and demanding. I haven't time for that, and it wasn't part of the bargain.'

'You don't have to worry about me on that score,' she declared, piqued. 'I won't invade your space, and I'd prefer a little around me too.'

'Remember you said that,' he warned her ominously. And then he began to touch and caress her again, in every place and every way he had already learned pleased her, arousing and awakening her so that she cried out involuntarily, unable to suppress the enormity of her desire, making nonsense, at that moment, of all she just said, as she surrendered herself to him utterly. Her body was still shuddering with the aftermath of pleasure when he said, quite calmly, 'It's only sex, Marissa. Don't forget it.'

It seemed to Marissa that it was quite a lot. Something irreversible had happened to her, for better or worse, and she could do no other than go along with it. And after a day or two of such deep, physical absorption that they needed little else, it was as if a veil had been drawn aside, allowing them to reach one another in other ways.

They emerged into the breathless, sunlit world outside and discovered it anew, really looking, this time, seeing wildlife and flowers and architecture, tasting the many-flavoured Provençal food with fresh enjoyment, sharing their preferences and discussing their differences with interest.

It was possible, now, to talk about the lives they had lived before they met. She told him about growing up at Grafton Court, her vague memories of her Welsh mother, going away to school, and then the awfulness of her father's remarriage to a woman who did not like her or want her around. He talked of a childhood fraught with financial perils, of his determination to ensure he never experienced such insecurity again, of the long, hard struggle to the top, a battle he still did not feel able to stop fighting.

He would not tell her any more about the woman he had once loved, but in many other ways Marissa felt she knew the determined boy who had come up the hard way and meant to stay king of the roost. And on his second visit to Aqua Parc she went with him, paced the site at his side as he spelled out the improvements and changes he planned, offering her comments and opinions freely.

'All good things come to an end eventually, Marissa,' he said to her one morning over breakfast, and when she looked at him blankly, he went on, 'We can't stay here any longer. Already I've taken more time than I should have. There are matters I have to attend to personally. How about dinner at the Negresco, by way of a final fling?'

'That would be lovely.' Marissa had never eaten at the opulent hotel on the Promenade des Anglais at Nice, once the favoured refuge of European royalty. But did he have to refer to their departure as 'the end'? she wondered. They were closer, now, than they had ever been, and she was light years away from the nervous girl who had come down on the sleeper express. Sexually, she was fulfilled and liberated as she had never dreamed she might be, and she was inspired by the ambition to make Rick's home and his life richer and fuller by her own efforts. Surely this was a sound basis on which their marriage could prosper?

She smiled at him.

'It will be good to be home,' she promised.

'Oh, I'm sure it will,' was all he said, suavely, and quite unrevealingly. The alarms should have sounded then, but Marissa, dangerously on the way to falling in love with this man she had married, was in no state to hear them.

Summer had come to Herefordshire when they got back. The land was a symphony of red, green, and blue—soil, crops, and brilliant sky, the air fragrant with the scent of hops, fruit heavy on the trees.

'I'll swear this county has the biggest bees anywhere!' laughed Marissa, as one zoomed past the car.

'That one's a kamikaze—intent on committing suicide on the windscreen,' Rick observed wryly.

They crested the rise of Sheep Hill, past the manicured green of the golf course, and Marissa's heart swelled with the joy of homecoming as she saw it all unfold before her...Bishopswell, with its grey church spire thrusting confidently into the blue sky, its black and white timbered houses clustering around it like chicks nestling up to the mother hen, and snug in its valley, Grafton Court, dreaming as it had for centuries amid the fields and woods. It was a view which never failed to make her catch her breath whenever she saw it, especially when returning after a long absence, and impulsively she closed her hand over Rick's, where it rested on the steering wheel.

'Happy?' he queried lightly, and with just the slightest edge to his voice, which she was too overcome by emotion to notice.

'Oh, yes! Yes!' she exclaimed. How could she be otherwise? To be coming back to this, her own special kingdom, and with him at her side to share it—it was going to be wonderful, she was convinced.

Mrs Reed was at the door to meet them, all smiles, as they drew up outside.

'Oh, Miss Marissa, it's so good to have you back! You look so well!' she cried happily. 'And Mr Jablonski—so brown you are! Everything's ready here, the bed's been aired, and all the workmen are out at last, thank goodness!'

The subtle difference hit Marissa the moment she stepped inside, and followed her wherever she went. It was still Grafton Court, essentially unchanged, but something which had become almost part of its fabric over the last few years had gone, was banished...that creeping, melancholy air of stealthily advancing decay.

The wooden floors had been cleaned and french polished so that they gleamed a dozen shades of gold. The roof had been mended, the plastering repaired, so there were no longer any telltale patches of damp. Old carpets had been professionally cleaned until the colours glowed, jewel-like, and, where this was not possible, they had been sympathetically replaced by new ones that blended superbly. And when summer had gone, carefully installed, unobtrusive central heating would ensure their comfort. There would be no more cold corners to shiver in. The house had been brought back to vibrant life, like the Sleeping Beauty.

'Not bad, eh?' grinned Rick, seeing her astonished, delighted expression. 'Neither should it be, since it cost a minor fortune.'

'Rick, it's...it's indescribable!' she exclaimed, dropping her bag and flinging her arms round him.

'Hey, what's that thing you said to me when I kissed you in front of Marie-Laure?' he said, startled.

Marissa giggled.

'Oh, that! "*Pas devant les domestiques*",' she told him. 'But this is different. Mrs Reed is hardly a *domestique*! She's practically family. Oh, and look, here's Idris! Here, boy!'

She released him and dropped to her knees as the sheepdog careened down the corridor towards her, tail thumping madly, body quivering ecstatically. 'Now I know I'm home!'

'Well, that puts *me* in my place!' Rick said

laconically, looking down indulgently at his wife's dark head as her arms went round her old dog. 'Guess she was yours first, old boy!'

Laughing, close to tears, Marissa happened to lift her head, and from this angle she was gazing through the open door into the drawing-room...where she could see something she had never expected to see again.

Still only half believing it, she disentangled herself from Idris and jumped to her feet. Her heart seemed to have all but stopped.

'It's Mother's piano!' she exclaimed, in a small, strangled voice. Closer inspection confirmed that it was, indeed, and there, too, was the little Georgian table. She ran from room to room, crying out with amazement as she found all the old pieces of furniture Vicky had sold, all back in their original places, as if they had never been removed.

Rick followed her slowly into the hall.

'You bought them all back,' she said, her eyes brimming. 'Oh, Rick, thank you! What a lovely surprise!'

'Correction—I bought them all in the first place, when Vicky put them up for auction,' he said quietly.

Marissa stood perfectly still, staring at him, while something clicked in her brain, leaving her cold and clear of sentimentality.

'It was you who bought them?' she said. 'Vicky never told me that.'

'Vicky didn't know. I did it anonymously,' he told her.

She frowned.

'I don't understand. Why didn't you tell me?' she demanded.

'Perhaps because you didn't ask,' he pointed out. 'For heaven's sake, Marissa, cut out the third degree! It just seemed to me that the old stuff belonged here, that's all. Aren't you glad to see it back? Your first reaction seemed to indicate that you were.'

'Yes. Of course,' she said stiltedly.

But she was remembering another day, the day when she had watched it all being carried out to the auctioneer's van, the awful row she'd had with Vicky afterwards, and the terrible sense of finality it had left her with. As if she had been orphaned, left entirely alone in the world, with no one to turn to…except…

That was the day she had come to her decision to marry Rick, and it was precisely that sequence of events which had pushed her over the brink into that hard-fought decision. And yet he had known, before he went away, and could have spared her that heartache. He had already made the crucial purchase, and had deliberately kept his action from her.

And now he stood there, smiling with complacent satisfaction, as if she should be so overwhelmed with gratitude that she remained unaware of having been manipulated.

That night, in the master bedroom which was now theirs, he made love to her with what she now recognised as skilful thoroughness, ensuring that she was denied nothing, exacting from her the same fierce, passionate response she could not suppress. But even as she cried out with pleasure at his touch, the little voice was back, talking to her in a cold, clear region of her mind which sensation did not reach.

Remember it's only sex, Marissa. He knows all too well how to reduce you to a trembling mass of female flesh, but it's a technique he could use with equal ease on any other woman's body, not exclusively yours.

She did not, now, have the strength to refuse him when he took her in his arms, but always there would be the painful knowledge that the choice she thought she had reached of her own accord had been subtly...and intentionally...influenced by his action. He had underhandedly subverted her free will.

In the morning, she noted that his flight bag was already packed.

'You didn't tell me you were going away so soon,' she said. 'Of course, I do realise that I didn't ask. Won't you tell me anything unless I put in a written request?'

'Holland. I'll be gone four or five days.' He sounded a bit short-tempered, but did not otherwise react to her acid tone. 'I've left a list of people I want you to invite for the weekend, when I get back. They're important, Marissa, so the full works, please.'

Yes, sir, she thought wryly, as he favoured her with a preoccupied smile, his mind already gone on ahead, working out some deal, she supposed. It was difficult to imagine the things they had done together, a few hours earlier, and her pulse quickened at the memory. But Rick certainly wasn't thinking about them, that was for sure. Had the honeymoon novelty of her body worn off so quickly? she wondered. Was that what he had meant when he said that it was only sex, that his interest in her might not long outlast her Provençal suntan?

But she had made a pact, and was obliged to keep her side of it. Marissa got on the telephone and was charming to the wives and secretaries of the people he had asked her to invite. She checked the stocks of drink, and planned menus with Mrs Reed, allocated rooms and saw that every comfort would be provided.

Meanwhile, she rode Salome, went for long walks with only Idris for company, visited people she knew in and around the village, and took what solace she could from the ever-present beauty and familiarity of her home and the countryside around it. This, at least, was always here, and could be trusted never to fail her, she thought, the one constant in her life.

Perhaps when Rick got home things would be better, she told herself. Perhaps she would have got over the hurt of feeling that she had been used, that she was really no more to him than a pretty face and a stylish social organiser. That, after all, was what he had married her for, and she had agreed those terms. She was not in love with him, and it was foolish to have invested so much emotion in a few days of sexual infatuation. It was time to get back to the cool, businesslike attitude with which they had first approached this marriage of convenience.

The weekend guests were due to arrive on Friday night...an American banker and his wife, an influential property dealer, and his, and Rick's brother Janusz, who would be alone, since his wife was back in the States and unable to get away for family reasons.

Rick was supposed to be home some time during the afternoon, and Marissa was on tenterhooks all day, strung out with anticipation, and determinedly telling herself every five minutes to play it cool.

But shortly after lunch he phoned her to say that his flight had been delayed, and he had no idea when he would manage to get away.

'You'll just have to keep them entertained,' he said, sounding distant and irritated. 'Hopefully, I'll make it some time this evening. It might be less difficult if we didn't live so far out in the sticks.'

'Well, that was *your* choice,' Marissa retorted angrily. 'I just went with the house!'

She slammed the phone down, already regretting the outburst. So much for keeping her cool! The evening had better be a success, she thought grimly, with or without Rick's presence!

She calmed herself down with a long, leisurely soak in the bath, and afterwards, while she was in her bedroom dressing to receive her guests, Mrs Reed tapped on her door.

'Mr Rick's brother phoned while you were in the bath,' she said. Already he was 'Mr Rick', no longer a formal 'Mr Jablonski', Marissa noted ruefully. 'He said to tell you he'd be bringing a lady guest after all. He did seem rather anxious to talk to you himself, but I could hardly drag you out of the bathroom, could I?' she added worriedly.

'No, you couldn't—it will be all right, I'm sure,' Marissa agreed. 'So long as it's no problem for you, and we do have a spare bedroom ready, don't we, since the lady isn't Mrs Janusz.' She grinned. Rick's brother had struck her as a solid family man, but you never could tell! However, he and the lady would be given separate rooms, since it wasn't for her to assume a more intimate relationship existed. Surely, even if he were playing around on the side, he wouldn't bring his girlfriend to a gathering where his brother would be present…and, no doubt, business would be talked over a spot of fishing, or riding!

After a warm, settled spell, the weather had turned cool and drizzly, and Marissa ordered log fires lit in the dining- and drawing-rooms, running the central heating in the bedrooms for an hour or two to counteract the slight chill in the air. Great cut glass bowls of roses stood on the tables, lamps glowed softly and the house was warm and welcoming as the guests arrived.

Nevertheless, the banker's wife, a rather unpleasant specimen of womanhood, who was wearing a thin, revealing gown more suited to Florida than Herefordshire, shivered through the cocktails and complained continuously that she found England cold and only half civilised. Her husband seemed annoyed by Rick's absence, in spite of Marissa's reasonable explanations—after all, anyone who flew regularly must understand about airport delays. She had to spend a fair amount of time and effort on placating him, while also entertaining the property man, who was dour and gloomy, and his wife, ensuring that no one was neglected. Jan was late too, just when she could have done with his help in talking to these rather difficult strangers.

At last she heard him arrive, and, excusing herself, hurried out to greet him and his unexpected guest. She was unprepared for the way Jan's resemblance to his brother hit her square in the chest, making her catch her breath as if in sudden pain.

'Marissa!' He kissed both her cheeks affectionately. 'You look fantastic—no need to ask how the honeymoon went!' He turned to the woman at his side, who was surveying Marissa with frank interest. 'This is Helena Giering. She turned up unexpectedly in England, and couldn't wait to meet you.'

She was tall, tanned and fair, with a strong, lively, mobile face, and long, disorderly blonde locks, an Amazon of a woman who radiated a vibrant personality.

'So you're Rick's wife!' Her voice was low and resonant. 'Congratulations, my dear! I never thought any woman would hook him, now! However did you manage it?'

Marissa was slightly alarmed by this unabashed forthrightness, although her first reaction was to find Helena Giering distinctive and likeable.

'You know Rick?' she asked faintly, and Helena gave her throaty laugh.

'Oh, for years—the families, you know. We aren't related, but in a Polish community everyone knows everyone!' she declared. 'I browbeat Jan into bringing me along with him—the poor man didn't really have any choice, so I just hope that's all right by you?'

'Of course. Any friend of Rick's is welcome here,' Marissa said at once, and truly, this tall Valkyrie's warmth and directness seemed to make her an ally with whom to face the rather frosty atmosphere back in the drawing-room. 'He isn't here yet—his flight was delayed—but he should be home later, and I'm sure he'll be glad to see you.'

After that, the evening was easier. Helena had not met the other guests previously, but they were all Americans, and she found things to talk about which related to them all. Jan was a great help too, as the men were able to talk business preliminaries over the drinks. By the time they moved into the dining-room—Marissa having decided she could not hold up dinner any longer—she had begun to relax a little. Even the banker's wife looked a little less disapproving under the influence of double Bourbons with which Jan had charmingly plied her.

Helena nudged Marissa's elbow under the table.

'I should go easy on the wine with old sourpuss over there,' she murmured, smiling broadly as if she and Marissa were merely exchanging pleasantries. 'She'll be two thirds cut before we get to the dessert!'

Marissa fought to repress a giggle. Helena was candid, impossible, and thoroughly engaging. All it required now was for Rick to turn up in a half-way cheerful mood, and the weekend would be off to a promising start.

They were in the drawing-room, drinking coffee, when he finally did arrive. Marissa heard Mrs Reed opening the front door, and she found her own hands clenching tightly with a tension she could not ignore. The house seemed to spring to life with his presence, and so did she.

'Glad you could all make it, folks,' he said, smiling expansively around the room. 'I'm sorry I'm a bit late, but you know how it is.'

And then—'Helena?' Marissa heard a cautious surprise in his voice, and something else, something curious and strange that made her own nerves sing with alarm, like a harshly plucked guitar.

Helena Giering stood up and went across the room to him, quite easily, naturally, and without embarrassment. She reached up both hands, clasping them at the back of his neck, kissed him first on one cheek, then the other.

'Ryszek,' she said, in that throatily vibrating voice of hers, 'that was very naughty of you, to get married when I wasn't around, but see, I brought myself along to meet your wife, and she's charming, very lovely.'

She released him from her close embrace, but stood with her arm loosely round his waist, while he had one hand on her shoulder, looking down at her. Marissa could not see the expression on his face, but for herself, she felt like an exhibit in a museum, being admired and assessed. It was not a feeling she enjoyed. Her eyes caught Jan's across the room; he looked uneasy, trying to signal something to her. An apology? An explanation?

And then it hit her. Helena wasn't just an old friend of Rick's, a family acquaintance going back years. Everyone in that circle had been at the wedding, and so would she have been, if that was all there was to it. But she wasn't there, because Rick had not invited her, and Marissa was instinctively sure she knew why. They had been something much closer than friends. Helena must be the woman Rick had once wanted to marry!

Marissa looked at them now, arms casually around one another, not obscenely or suggestively, but unmistakably two people who knew one another extremely well. We parted friends, he had said. She didn't believe it. She didn't believe they had parted at all. Helena might once have refused to marry him, but it seemed to Marissa that they were still lovers!

All that nonsense about not giving second chances, she thought disgustedly, would only fool someone gullible, as Rick had obviously thought *she* was. This way, he got to have his cake and eat it. He had her, Marissa, to run Grafton Court and provide his entrée into English country society, while still maintaining his relationship with Helena.

No wonder Helena was so friendly towards her, and behaved quite naturally, not at all hurt by Rick's marriage. She recognised it for what it was, a sham, a charade, a PR exercise which made no difference to what the two of them had going between them.

The conversation was flowing around her, people were laughing and drinking their coffee, while she sat like a wooden statue, alone with the awful thoughts in her head. She got up, mechanically, excusing herself as if she had to go to the kitchen.

She was aware of Rick's eyes following her—he had not spoken directly to her since he arrived—but it was Jan who followed her out into the kitchen.

'Marissa!'

She turned, facing him, not really wanting to hear what she knew he was going to tell her. His eyes were concerned, his voice gentle.

'I didn't really think it a good idea to bring Helena with me, but she's a very forceful lady,' he said. 'I wanted to talk to you first, but you weren't available when I phoned.'

Marissa shrugged.

'It's all right, I get the picture,' she said.

'I don't think you do. We were all friends as kids, Rick, myself, Helena and her sister Danuta. When Helena's husband died, I guess Rick saw her through the worst of it. I'm sure it was all over long before he married you.'

So Helena had not only turned Rick down, but

married someone else! The bond between them must be even stronger than she had thought, to have survived all that. She was grateful to Rick's brother for trying to reassure her, and maybe he even believed what he had just told her, but she was not convinced.

'I think Helena would like very much for you and her to be friends,' Rick continued earnestly. 'Not that you'll see much of her—she isn't in England very often. She runs her own business and leads a very full life.'

'She seems very pleasant,' said Marissa. 'Actually, I rather like her.' Which was true, and confusing, and didn't help at all, she realised. 'I must go, Jan. I have to have a word with Mrs Reed.'

'And with your husband, I hope,' he reminded her. 'I get the feeling all isn't well between you two, and I just hope that I'm wrong.'

'Everything's fine,' Marissa assured him automatically.

She only wished that it were. No jealousy—it's not part of the bargain, he had insisted. No emotional involvement. Just a straight business arrangement, which, unfortunately, they had complicated by trying to mix it with sex!

And now she found herself married to a man who had a lover of some years' standing in his life! Tonight, in a few hours' time, she would be expected to share his bed, and, since he'd been away for the best part of a week, he would probably want to make love. Marissa blinked quickly and tried to steady her erratic breathing. Could she ever tremble with pleasure in his arms again?

Or—what was probably a harder question—could she teach herself to live without that pleasure?

CHAPTER NINE

IT WAS late when the gathering broke up, and Marissa did not retire to her bedroom until she knew all her guests had settled down for the night. Then she had to speak to Mrs Reed about early-morning tea and coffee, and breakfast, and it was after midnight when she finally climbed the stairs.

Now—the moment she had been dreading. Did she pretend all was well, go along with the notion that Helena was just an old friend who had unexpectedly turned up? And if she tacitly accepted the situation now, was she signifying her willingness to go on doing so? How would she react when Rick kissed her...touched her?

But when she opened the door, quietly, she saw that Rick was already in bed, and lying on his back, fast asleep. Well, he'd had a busy week, and a tiring day hanging around airports, then come home to play obliging host to a houseful of guests. It was not surprising that he was exhausted. Marissa stood for a moment looking down at his face, the deep furrows along his forehead, the combative mouth drawn into a still line by sleep, and wondered why she felt so empty and bereft. He had, after all, allowed her a reprieve. Switching off the bedside lamp at his side, she crawled into bed and lay coldly hunched at her own side, listening to him breathe, and wondering whether sleep would ever come to her.

It did, eventually, and when she woke she found that she was alone in bed. She rubbed her eyes blearily, saw that it was only seven o'clock, but could not call sleep back.

She got up, drew the curtains, and then she saw them: Rick and Helena. They were walking across the grass towards the house, deep in conversation. Helena laughed, gave him an affectionate push, and he ruffled her already untidy hair in retaliation. Marissa dropped her hand from the curtain and drew back, icy cold.

Did he love Helena, then? A woman who had turned him down once, married someone else, and wasn't prepared to give up the 'full life' she led to minister to a man's needs, even his? I'm second-best, Marissa thought, just someone he found to fill the bill.

They were in the dining-room when she went down, half an hour later. She heard their voices from the corridor, but they were talking Polish, which was still a closed book to Marissa, although the pace and flow of their discussion sounded animated and involved.

'Good morning,' she said, as evenly as she could, but she had to admit that her own voice sounded stilted and unnatural.

'Hi,' Rick said cheerfully. 'You looked as if you were out for the count when I woke up, so I didn't disturb you. Anyhow, I wanted to have a chat with Helena.'

I'll bet you did, Marissa thought acidly, sitting down and helping herself to coffee.

'We went for a long walk, up…what was it called, Ryszek…Sheep's Hill,' said Helena, brimming with enthusiasm and obviously not at all disconcerted by Marissa's presence. 'It's heavenly up there...and the views! You grew up in this house, I understand.'

'That's right,' Marissa answered faintly. This woman was open and friendly, but was it possible for them to share the same man, and remain amicable? 'My family has lived here for four hundred years.'

'Like your grandfather and his place in Poland, eh, Ryszek?' Helena said, smiling. 'No wonder you feel so much at home in this atmosphere. It must be in the blood.'

Marissa's mouth dropped open. She stared bemusedly at Rick, and although she said nothing, her astonishment was plainly written on her face for the American woman to see.

'He didn't tell you about that? Ryszek, that was very bad of you!' Helena slapped his wrist lightly with her folded napkin, and turned back to Marissa. 'His grandfather had acres of land and a big country house. And a title to go with it, apparently. Of course, it all went...the war and everything, you know.'

Rick returned Marissa's accusing gaze with a nonchalant grin, and raised his broad shoulders in a shrug. She remembered the odd intimations she had had about him, from time to time, which had proven to be right. Yet he had let her call him an ignorant peasant, or words to that effect, and never troubled to tell her that his ancestry was at least a match for hers!

'I never saw any of this, of course, so it's all totally irrelevant,' he said.

Irrelevant or not, he could have told her! She

recalled those long evenings at harbourside cafés in Provence, when they had talked endlessly about themselves...or at least, she had. He, it seemed, had only given her what snippets of information he'd considered unimportant enough to reveal to her. There had been no real confidences, no genuine sharing of themselves. It had all meant very little, after all. '*It's only sex, Marissa.*' And that, indeed, was all it turned out to have been, she reflected wretchedly.

From there, she felt the day, her marriage, the entire situation slipping away from her, beyond a point where she had any sensible control over any of them, and could only coast along, a helpless spectator. She went through the motions—ordered meals, served drinks, made conversation, kept everyone happy with the long-practised social skills which, fortunately, worked of their own volition, and did not desert her now.

With Rick, she was as polite and amiable as she could possibly be...perhaps a little too courteous for a normal husband/wife relationship, which was the front she was supposed to present. She couldn't help it. Every time she looked at Rick, she seemed to intercept him smiling, naturally and easily, at Helena, and in her mind the scene would extend itself so that she saw him kissing her...saw them entwined, making love...and she found herself trying to work out the times when both of them had been out of her sight, and wondering if they had had long enough to snatch a short while together. It would be done very discreetly and circumspectly, she had no doubt. It was in Rick's interest to maintain the status quo as it was, not to upset it.

The poison worked slowly and steadily in her all

day, and late in the afternoon, when her guests were resting in their rooms, she slipped quietly upstairs to her bedroom. Without putting it into precise words, in her head she had reached a decision...more an instinctive reaction than a reasoned one, but the result was the same.

She could not continue to share a bed with Rick. If she did, and he touched her, as he most certainly would, she knew she would not have the strength to refuse him. Her senses were too easily swayed by him, and it would happen, inevitably. She would let him make love to her, and afterwards she would hate herself, and him too.

No matter what she told herself about business arrangements without emotional strings, it was no good—she simply was not sophisticated enough to sleep with a man who came to her from another woman's bed.

She had no idea where Rick was—he could well be in Helena's arms right now—but in his absence she worked quickly and mechanically, transferring her clothes and possessions from their room back to the one she had occupied before her marriage. Soon it was as if she had never been there.

She was just removing the last of her cosmetics from the top of the dressing-table when the door opened softly. Without turning, she felt his eyes on her, and a ripple of nervous fear trembled along her spinal cord.

'Marissa?' His voice was quiet, but none the less authoritative. 'What exactly are you doing?'

She forced herself to turn and face him calmly, looking into the cold, dispassionate sea-green eyes which still watched her closely.

'I'm moving back into my old room,' she told

him quietly. 'I've thought about it, and come to the conclusion that you were right when you said I wasn't ready for...for this close a relationship. I'd like to...to back off a little, keep it strictly business.'

'Hm.' He did not move, nor did his eyes leave her, or alter their unrevealing expression. 'It's a bit like splitting the atom and then trying to pretend you never did, isn't it? Is it possible to go back, in that way? We *have* been lovers...many times, and very thoroughly and enjoyably. Or so it appeared.'

Marissa moistened her dry lips nervously with her tongue.

'So once a man and woman have slept together, are you saying that the sexual relationship is bound to continue indefinitely?' she challenged.

A hint of an icy smile touched his lips.

'In marriage, that's usually the case,' he replied drily.

And outside it too, thought Marissa, remembering Helena.

'In marriage, people don't usually hide things from one another,' she retorted. On the brink of telling him what she knew, something made her draw back. Could she even live with him, when she had admitted she was aware he had another woman? She'd have to leave him, and that was a step too final and enormous for her to contemplate. Instead she quickly changed tack.

'You never told me anything about the place your grandfather owned in Poland, or the fact that your family were titled,' she accused him.

Rick shrugged.

'All that old family history?' he said, as if amazed she should consider it important. 'It's all in the past. To be honest, I never gave it a thought. I'm an American, Marissa, for all I'm proud of my Polish ancestry. I've made it on my own merit. If that's not good enough for you—well, it's just too bad.'

He opened the door wider, and a dismissive gesture of his hand told her she was free to go...indeed, ushered her out.

'Don't let me keep you,' he said coolly. 'And Marissa, there's no need for you to lock your door. If I were desperate to get in, it certainly wouldn't stop me, and I'm not in the habit of forcing myself on women.'

She was trembling as she reached the sanctuary of her old room. It had been both harder and easier than she had expected, and she wondered if, in her heart, she had wanted him to forbid, protest, take her in his arms and use the one means of persuasion which would not have failed. She should have known him better than that, proud, stubborn, stiff-necked devil that he was! Why should he go to so much trouble when he really didn't need her all that badly?

And now she had to play the role she had been bought and paid for. She had to dress and look beautiful and behave charmingly to these strangers in her home. To laugh and smile and make them feel welcome, so that whatever deal Rick was trying to pull off, now or in some Machiavellian future only he had thought out, would be eased by her warmth and courteous sociability.

Then, after carrying out this purpose for which she suddenly had no heart at all, she had to come back to this room and lie alone in this narrow bed, bereft of the touch of his knowing hands, and the sound of his laughter in the darkness.

Well, at least her moving out had made it easier for him and Helena, she thought wryly, as she started to apply her make-up.

She thought the torture of that weekend would never come to an end, but it did, at last. The banker and the property man, together with their respective wives, left on Sunday night after dinner, with Marissa smiling until she felt her face cracking with the effort as she wished them goodbye.

'You can finalise that business in Holland now, Jan,' Rick said to his brother as they all sat in the drawing-room having a final nightcap. He turned almost formally to Marissa. 'I have to go away again for a few days, tomorrow.'

She started.

'Already? Where are you going this time?' she enquired.

'I shall be moving around, so I'm afraid I can't tell you exactly,' he said. 'I'll be in touch with you and let you know when I'll be back. Helena——' warmth returned to his voice as he spoke to *her*, 'I can take you to the airport, if that's any help to you, but I'll be leaving very early.'

'Lovely—no problem,' she said, with her expansive smile. 'I'll turn in now, and set my alarm so that I don't delay you.'

Marissa listened to this little charade, sickened. She was almost inclined to tell them that they really did not have to keep up this ridiculous pretence on *her* account. She knew very well that they would spend the night in the same bed—well, why not, since Rick was under no obligation, now, to sleep with his wife? And if they wanted to take off for a few days together, there was very little she could do about it. She'd married him, he'd kept his side of the agreement, and she had Grafton Court. He'd promised her nothing else, certainly not fidelity, so how could she turn around now and demand it?

After they had all left, everything was still the same. The old house still dreamed peacefully as the sunshine returned, the apples ripened on countless acres of trees, a blue haze softened the outline of the distant Welsh mountains. It was all here, all she had ever wanted, all hers, no matter what happened. Then why did she feel so sour, so dispirited, so hurt? Why was it no longer enough?

For three days Marissa moped about like this. There was no word from Rick, although she watched for the post, and jumped every time the telephone rang. And finally a kind of rebellion shook her.

I'm a young and beautiful woman, she thought, eyeing her reflection without vanity, but with no false modesty, either. Why should I sit here and wait for the imperial command of a man who's spending his time with another woman? I promised to be here to organise parties and to charm his business acquaintances, but not to sit on my backside, twiddling my thumbs while he amuses himself elsewhere. Two could play at that game!

She packed a bag, left the shiny new sports car Rick had bought for her use standing in the garage, and caught the train to London. It never occurred to her to take refuge in her father's new house in Cheltenham. They had spoken briefly on the phone once or twice since she had come back from France, but she didn't want Vicky's alert, malicious brain cottoning on delightedly to the fact that already her marriage had hit trouble.

Bunty, her ex-flatmate, was pleased to see her when she landed on the doorstep, but doubtful about putting her up.

'There's Jo, you see, the girl who took your place—she has your old room,' she explained. 'Besides, why are you so set on slumming? I'd have thought Mrs Rick Jablonski could have hired the Ritz for the night!'

So it was true, Marissa thought disconsolately, coming suddenly into money *did* distance you from old friends, even when that was the last thing you wanted. She was no longer one of them.

'It would only be for a couple of nights.' she said in a small voice. 'I don't mind sleeping on the couch. I don't want to go to a hotel, where I wouldn't know anyone.'

Bunty relented at once.

'I'm sorry, Marissa—I just didn't think of it that way,' she said. 'Of course you're welcome to stay—we'll manage. A crowd of us are going out to a club tonight, dancing. Why don't you come along?'

'I'd like to...but I don't want to be a spare part,' Marissa said doubtfully.

'Don't be silly, it's not like that. It won't be all couples,' Bunty assured her. 'There's Sally and Michelle, remember, and Jake, who worked with you on that lipstick ad. He's bringing his friend Graham. Come on, you didn't come to London to sit and watch telly, did you? I'm sure your husband won't mind, if you're with old friends.'

'He won't care in the least,' Marissa said firmly. In fact, Rick wouldn't give a damn where she was, what she did, or with whom, so long as she was back at Grafton Court when he required her presence.

She stiffled a dull ache inside her, just below her breastbone, as she threw herself into getting ready for an evening out.

It seemed an age since she was free and single, leading this kind of life, although it was really only a few short months. The bright disco lights, the crowds of laughing, flamboyantly dressed young people, buying drinks and chatting one another up…Marissa knew a moment of pure panic, feeling as out of place as if she'd strayed into a tribal rite in a Zulu village.

Oh, come on, you're only twenty-two, not an old married lady who hasn't been out of the house at night in years, she told herself scornfully. All the same, it felt weird, and to compensate she found herself drinking a little more than usual, talking and laughing more loudly, dancing more frenetically.

'You're a great girl, Marissa!' Jake's friend Graham shouted above the music as they danced. 'If I were your husband, I'd keep you strictly to myself!'

'We have an understanding,' Marissa giggled. Graham was amusing and attractive, a great dancer, and his obvious admiration did wonders for her wounded feelings. As the music slowed and the lights dimmed, he gathered her closer to him, holding her more tightly, his mouth against her hair.

Why not? she thought recklessly. If he asks me…and he will…why shouldn't I? It was no more than Rick was doing. If he wanted a marriage of convenience he could have one, but both partners played by the same ground rules. If *he* could have lovers, why couldn't she? Serve him right!

'Marissa,' her partner murmured in her ear, 'it's getting too crowded in here…I'd much rather be alone with you. Let's get a taxi and go to my place.'

His hand worked its way down her back towards her hips, forcing her body to his, and he began to kiss her neck in the semi-darkness, while all around them entwined couples did the same. A sudden deep-seated nausea welled up in Marissa's throat—disgust with herself, revulsion, and a deep, deep, despair, because she knew she couldn't, just couldn't go on with this.

'No…please let me go…!' she cried, fighting to free herself from the strength of his all too evident arousal. Wrenching herself free, she pushed her way through the crowd of gyrating dancers until she reached the relative calm of the brightly lit ladies' cloakroom.

She stared at herself in the mirror—the much admired and photographed Marissa Beaumont Jablonski, her hair awry, her mascara smudged, her eyes wide and full of newly discovered wretchedness.

She couldn't go home with Graham or any other man and let him make love to her, not even out of a vengeful desire to pay Rick back in his own coin. The very thought was enough to make her feel ready to throw up. She wanted only Rick to touch her, wanted to lie only in *his* arms, hearing *his* voice, seeing his now heart-wrenchingly familiar craggy face when she woke in the mornings. Talking to him, arguing with him, loving him…

Loving him. That was it, that was where she had gone wrong. She had married him in cold blood—or so she thought—and without ever meaning to, without knowing until this moment that it had happened, she had fallen in love with him. How unutterably foolish of her, because from this totally unexpected point she had no idea where to go.

She went back to Grafton Court, because it was home, because she had nowhere else, went back like an injured fox crawling into its lair. And because, in spite of everything, she was full of a fierce need to see Rick again.

Not that she had any idea at all of how she intended to behave towards him when he did turn up. She could hardly confess to him that she had broken the terms of their agreement, and fallen in love. No jealousy, no emotional strings. Not only did he not love her, there was another woman in his life.

The only way she could keep him was to accept the situation as it was, pretending that it didn't trouble her. Since she could not crawl back cravenly into his bed, begging him to take up where they left off, that meant she must face a future of being his wife and yet not his wife. Longing for him and trying not to show it, trying to be satisfied with his occasional platonic presence in her life.

Could she endure that? The alternative was to leave him, and that was …unthinkable.

'You're hardly eating anything, Miss Marissa,' Mrs Reed said reproachfully. 'You're that thin, just like you were when you came back from Africa with that bug. All eyes and hair, you are! Mr Rick will have my guts for garters for starving you, when he gets home!'

Marissa smiled wanly.

'No one could starve here, the amount of food you put out, unless it was from choice,' she said. 'I've always been slim, you know that.'

'Slim, not skinny. There's a difference,' the

housekeeper retorted worriedly. 'You'll start losing it from all the wrong places, and men don't like that! I know it's not my business, but...'

For as long as Marissa could remember, Mrs Reed had used that introduction when she intended asking something deeply personal. She had been part of the household for so long that she felt able to do this with impunity. To forestall her, Marissa stood up quickly.

'I'm perfectly all right, Mrs Reed,' she said quickly. 'Just a little tired. London exhausted me—I'm not used to it any more. I know it's early, but I think I'll go to bed.'

She escaped swiftly to her bedroom. Mrs Reed knew very well that she and Rick slept separately, and Marissa did not want to touch on that subject—it was too private, too deeply humiliating and painful.

Removing her dress, she sat in her bra and slip, looking at herself in the mirror. Was it true she was losing her figure? Her breasts still had their former fullness, but there were little hollows at the base of her throat that she had not noticed before, and her face had shadows which made her cheekbones appear higher and more emphatic than ever.

Did it matter? She had been desirable to her husband only briefly, and it was over almost before it had properly begun. Picking up a hairbrush, she began to brush the long, glossy hair, watching with absent-minded detachment as it sprang back from the bristles into shiny, living waves.

The screech of a car's engine on the drive, the sweep of its headlamps across the window, startled her, and her heart began to expand behind its fragile cage of bone, threatening her survival. It was Rick, she knew the sound of the red convertible, but he did not usually drive so recklessly.

Turned to stone, Marissa sat, hairbrush in hand, listening as the front door was opened. The thud of his flight bag dropped heavily in the hall, Mrs Reed's words of welcome cut off brusquely by his hard, swift steps approaching up the staircase. Something had put him in a foul mood, no doubt about it.

I couldn't face him tonight, anyhow, Marissa thought, her mouth dry with nerves. As it was, he would go to the master bedroom and they would not meet until morning. Perhaps by then she would have composed herself, and he would have slept away his bad temper. The best she could hope for was that they could face one another across the breakfast table as two civilised human beings.

'Marissa! Where in hell are you?'

She froze still further. Rick's voice rang with a cold ferocity, as, without giving her time to answer, he slammed open the door to her room. In the mirror she saw his face, dark as thunder, brows drawn into angry lines, mouth thin-lipped and white with bottled-up fury.

Her heart thumped; between a treacherous joy at the sight of him, and fear of such a rage as she had never before known in him, she could hardly keep herself from shaking.

'For goodness' sake, Rick, what's wrong?' she asked, in a voice too deliberately light. 'You look as if you're about to commit murder!'

It was not a good choice of words. She saw him flex his hands, and knew, without having to ask, that his anger was beamed sharply and exclusively on her. Her breath came shortly, in ragged gasps of fear, and she dared not move, or even turn to face him.

'Well, maybe I am,' he said, slowly and heavily, in a voice thick with accusation. 'I just might kill you, lady, if you're not real careful! So don't push your luck!'

He closed the door behind him, sliding the bolt ominously, and advanced until he was standing right behind her, close enough to touch, his hands still tightly clenched.

'Perhaps you would like to tell me what you were doing in that nightclub, smooching all over some guy, letting him paw you!' he said with fierce disgust. Reaching into his pocket, he took out a photograph and tossed it carelessly on to the dressing-table in front of her. And there she was, with her arms around Graham, his hands clutching her buttocks and pressing her hips to his, his mouth nuzzling her neck.

'If that's what you're prepared to do in public, I'm not so sure I want to know what you let him do to you in private!' said Rick scathingly. 'Was it good, Marissa? Did you learn a few variations I didn't teach you? Or teach *him* a few, perhaps? Couldn't do without it, after all. *Could* you?'

CHAPTER TEN

HE WAS angry enough to kill her, and seconds earlier she had been gripped by fear that he might. But now his scorn and disgust produced a different reaction, and she turned to face him, jumping to her feet.

Her anger matched his as she said coldly, 'You're hardly in a position to criticise anything I do. I'm here when you need me to be, fulfilling the part you hired me to play. What I do with my own time is my business—as is yours. No strings, no emotional ties—remember?'

She could have said that it wasn't true, she'd done nothing with Graham apart from dance, and her flight to London had been caused by her pain at the realisation of Rick's own infidelity. But why should she beg and plead for his forgiveness? Let him think she had a lover, if he chose to. Certainly she would not allow him to realise that she cared for him!

He pointed accusingly at the photograph.

'It's my business what you do when *that* is the result. I have a right to demand a reasonable standard of decorum and discretion in *my* wife, especially in public. Your face is well known, Marissa, and so is my name. That picture was sent to me with a threat to have it printed in a certain salacious newspaper gossip column. I had to pay a large sum to prevent that happening. I don't enjoy being the subject of blackmail, and it isn't what I expected from you.'

Marissa was shocked by the revelation that someone

would go to such lengths for money, and that a casual night out, a little flirtatious dancing, could damage her husband's reputation so much that he was prepared to pay to suppress the evidence. It surely couldn't be *her* reputation that he cared about!

But she could not bring herself to back down and apologise now. Her only defence against him and her own fierce emotions was a surly defiance.

'What a pity!' she said, with heavy sarcasm. 'When you opened the package, the goods weren't what you ordered! Would you like to take me back to the shop and ask for a refund?'

She watched his eyes narrow, his face darken, and as she stared, mesmerised, into his furious, glacial eyes, the fear her anger had momentarily dispelled returned. Once she had thought that if she had Rick Jablonski on her side, she need be afraid of nothing else. But what happened to those who had him against them?

'You've no shame, have you?' he demanded. 'You need teaching a lesson you won't forget in a hurry!'

He shook off his jacket, tossing it carelessly on to the floor, and advanced towards her, unbuckling the leather belt of his trousers. Marissa gasped and backed away, convinced that he was about to use it to give her a thrashing, but there was no place for her to go, and his iron-hard hand seized her wrist as she bumped against the dressing table behind her.

'No use looking for an escape route, Marissa!' he said harshly, purposefully. 'There isn't one. Not this time!'

She screamed as he pushed her roughly on to the bed, but he clapped a hand over her mouth and forced her down, holding her rigidly with his knee between her legs. Too late, she saw that he didn't intend to beat her, that he had in mind a far more primitive and humiliating punishment. Desperate, she sank her teeth into his hand, but he only laughed humourlessly, as if the pain were nothing to him, and set about ripping away her thin undergarments as easily as if they had been paper.

'If you choose to leave my bed, that's your privilege,' he said, between grated teeth. 'But if *this* is what you need, don't go looking for it elsewhere!'

He took her savagely, without any tenderness or consideration, and although he had stripped her naked he only disarranged his own clothing as much as was strictly necessary. But a violent, female triumph surged in her at the very feel of him near her, inside her, as she had never expected him to be again, and she matched his ferocious lovemaking with a turbulent desire of her own, winding herself around him, clinging to him, hearing herself making sounds more animal than human. Spent and shuddering, she lay back, gasping with exertion and astounded by a shameful sensuality she had never suspected in herself.

Rick shook her off, almost disdainfully, and she watched wordlessly as he restored his clothes to immaculate order, picking up his jacket, scarcely looking at her as he did so. This was in no sense a reconciliation. She had transgressed and he had chastised her, and now he had no more emotion left for her than he would have had for a piece of flotsam cast up on a beach.

Mortified by his contemptuous treatment of her, and even more so by her own frenziedly uninhibited response, she said in a small, flat voice, 'So this is the man who never had to coerce a woman! In my book, that was practically rape!'

He cast one scornful glance at her as she lay on the bed, still breathing heavily, lips swollen, hair all over her face.

'If you think I forced you, you're fooling no one but

yourself,' he said scathingly, and closed the door firmly behind him as he left her.

For a long time Marissa did not move, but finally she crawled under the quilt, drew her chin to her knees, and curled herself into a tight little ball. She felt bruised and abused, but he was right, it had been nothing like rape. After the first shocked seconds, she had welcomed it, wanted it. Wanted him. And loved him now. Even though he had made it plain that to him she was no more than a possession to be kept in its place.

All through the night she tossed about, dozing sporadically, waking and reliving those violent moments with Rick, the shame and the pleasure, in equal parts. The gnawing agony of loving him, and the bitterness of knowing that beneath his disgust lay only indifference. He might have possessed her out of anger, and a desire to punish her for daring, as he thought, to step out of line, but for her as a person—as a woman—he did not care a jot. Well, hadn't she known that from the beginning? *She* was the one who had not kept to the terms.

A grey dawn was lightening the sky when she finally gave up all pretence of trying to sleep. She showered, dressed, went down to the stable, tacked up Salome and went for a long ride through the hushed, just awakening countryside. She felt desperately alone, for, having loved, she could not, now, confuse loneliness with solitude.

By the time she returned to the house she was sure in her mind of one thing. She could not live with a man she loved, who would never love her. A man who none the less insisted on a double standard—perfect behaviour from a woman for whom he did not care, and absolute freedom for himself.

She was drinking coffee and toying aimlessly with a piece of toast when Rick came into the dining-room.

Clean, freshly shaved, immaculately suited, he bore little resemblance to the furious savage in her bedroom last night. Only the icily hard eyes were the same, confirming that he felt no remorse, no softening in his attitude towards her.

He didn't sit down, just stood looking down at her, while Marissa stared back, and an awful sense of finality deepened between them.

'I don't know about you,' he said, 'but I reckon we should call it a day. It will be said we didn't give it enough time, but in business the knack is knowing when you've made a mistake and should cut your losses.'

She nodded numbly.

'I agree. I can't live with you, Rick. I wasn't what you needed, and perhaps it was a silly idea from the beginning.' She shrugged. 'Whatever arrangements you want to make, I'll go along with them.'

'Let the lawyers earn their money and sort it out.' he said distastefully, as if he had no desire other than to be done with her, as quickly as possible. 'I can afford the odd mistake. As for Grafton Court—it's yours. I shan't be here again, but I'll have the deed transferred to you.' Looking at her stunned, nonplussed expression, he essayed a wry smile. 'It's what you wanted. Isn't it?'

Marissa came back from modelling swimsuits in Australia aware that more than just jet-lag and the change from warmth and sunshine to a raw November cold was wrong with her. She had not felt well all the time they had been working. Her normal healthy appetite had deserted her, she had been nauseated by everyday things like cups of tea, only to wake in the night with wild, insensate cravings for exotica like pork satay, or fish fingers dipped in mayonnaise. Her bodily clock was ticking all awry, not functioning as it should, and what had been merely an awful suspicion when she left England was solidifying into inescapable fact. She had to be pregnant, and by her reckoning she must have conceived on that last, savagely passionate encounter with Rick, when they had lost all sense of reason or caution.

As she sat in the doctor's waiting-room, Marissa wondered wretchedly what she was going to do if the result was positive. She had returned to modelling the day after Rick had left her, and although the assignments had come quickly enough, pregnancy was going to make working difficult, if not impossible. She had found a small but pleasant flat, had enough money for her needs, but a baby was a different proposition, with an endless list of requirements…clothes, schools, a proper home to live in, a mother who was around most of the time, not on the other side of the world, or dashing from job to job.

The irony was that, although divorce proceedings were already in hand, a hefty allowance was paid into her bank account each month, where it remained, untouched. As would any financial settlement Rick chose to make on her, Marissa had decided. She might have been bought, but she refused to be paid off. And Grafton Court, which she had left the day after he did, remained, smoothly run by Mrs Reed and the staff, but otherwise unoccupied.

I'll never live here again, she had thought sadly, as she looked back from the bus as it crested the road by Sheep Hill. She had loved it all her life, and still did, but now, without Rick, it had become an empty shell she could not inhabit without seeing his face in every room, hearing his voice along every corridor.

Five minutes in the doctor's surgery overturned every notion in her head, and she came out hugging herself, wearing a silly smile on her tired but lovely face. She was indeed going to be a mother, and suddenly, now that it was fact, not mere suspicion, that knowledge put every other consideration starkly into perspective.

Walking down the grey, busy streets, swept by a chill north-wester, Marissa saw little of what was going on around her. I'm going to have a baby, she told herself over and over again, and the fear, now, was replaced by a sweet, secret delight. The problems would return, she knew, but she could not think of them right now. This was Rick's baby, the child they had made together—it had not, after all, been all for nothing.

And now you have to stop being silly and pig-headed and think of your child, instead of what *you* can't face, what gives *you* pain, what offends *your* pride, she admonished herself. By the time the baby was born, the divorce would be final, but both she and Rick were too well-known for the birth to be kept a secret. There was nowhere she could hide where he would not learn about it, no way either of them could escape the consequences of what they had done together.

She did not want his money, any of it, for herself, but her child had a right to a decent upbringing, and it would be wrong of her to salvage her own pride by denying him or her. A flicker of pain shot though her—Rick might easily refuse to believe the baby was his. Marissa straightened her shoulders. So be it. Her child, at least, was entitled to what *she* had had—a happy, healthy childhood at Grafton Court, growing up among the peaceful countryside and gentle-voiced people of rural Herefordshire. If Rick stopped every penny he was now attempting to pay her, on the grounds that he was not the father of her child, he couldn't take away the home he had returned to her, as he had promised. They could live there, not rich, but comfortable, she and her son...or daughter. They'd manage, somehow.

Marissa turned into Oxford Street, still oblivious of her surroundings, and bumped clumsily into a woman heading in the opposite direction.

'I'm sorry,' she said, attempting to sidestep, but the woman caught her arm, and the warm, throaty voice brought her back to the present reality with a jolt.

'Marissa! By all that's marvellous!'

Helena Giering wore a curly astrakhan coat trimmed with white fur, and a matching hat sat atop her disordered blonde hair. She was smiling, that open, friendly smile Marissa remembered from her fateful visit to Grafton Court—how *could* she! What a day, Marissa thought, to bump into your estranged husband's lover!

'Helena,' she said woodenly. 'How are you?'

'I'm fine, as always,' the other woman said breezily. 'But how about you—you look lovely, if a little run down.' She inspected Marissa critically.

'I'm all right. Look, I must fly,' Marissa said, anxious not to prolong this uncomfortable...for her, at least...encounter.

But Helena would not hear of it, and she could be extremely purposeful.

'Oh, you can't...I'm so glad we met!' she exclaimed. 'Let's have coffee. We can't stand here freezing.'

She drew Marissa into a coffee shop, and commandeered the waitress, in spite of there being several customers ahead of them. Marissa, actually, was quite glad to sit down, as a sudden wave of fatigue assailed her, but she wrinkled her nose at the scent of coffee. She had only just reached a point where she could drink it again without instantly feeling sick.

'Rick told me you two had split up,' Helena said, without preamble. 'He wouldn't say why, and that's odd, because since we were kids we've confided most things to one another. But when your name is mentioned, he just clams up.'

Marissa gave a small gasp of astonishment. This woman could not be for real! She seemed so genuinely concerned, and yet surely the break-up of Rick's marriage could not be bad news for her?

'I would have thought you'd be certain to know all about it,' she said coolly.

Helena frowned.

'Marissa, I *don't*. However, I have to say, I haven't seen Rick this trip. I phoned him, but he was in some meeting, and I have to go back to New York tomorrow, so I guess we won't actually get around to seeing each other.'

'You haven't seen him?' Marissa echoed. This much casualness between lovers was hard to understand. 'How can you be so nonchalant about it, Helena?' she burst our involuntarily. 'Don't you love him?'

Helena put her head on one side and gave a short, wry laugh.

'Adore him, darling, always have, but it's an old friendship, and will keep,' she said. 'Why are you looking at me like that, Marissa? Have I said something funny?'

'In a way. You're the oddest pair of lovers I've ever met,' Marissa declared. Seeing Helena's blank look, she said 'It's OK, you don't have to pretend. Rick told me that he once wanted to marry you, and you turned him down.'

'Rick *told* you that? Are you quite sure that's what he said?' Helena demanded, in an odd voice, which made Marissa look up questioningly.

'Well, not exactly, but he told me there was someone, and when you turned up at Grafton Court I put two and two together, and...'

Helena's long, fine-boned hand rested on her arm, its

pressure silencing her.

'Marissa, it wasn't me Rick wanted to marry. That was my sister Danuta, who now lives in Australia, with her husband—they run a multi-national conglomerate so vast I don't think even she knows how much they own.' she said. 'Although sometimes I reckon she still regrets not snapping up Rick when she had the chance! Oh, I admit, Rick and I had a bit of a fling, which went on for quite some years, in an on-and-off manner. I helped him over Danuta, he helped me over the loss of my husband. But there's been nothing between us—oh, not since long before Rick met you. Marissa—be careful!'

Marissa's cup had slipped from her hand, and coffee slopped all over the table, spilling down her coat and burning her hand. Helena called commandingly for the waitress, a cloth, and cold water, and such was her aura that she got all three, double quick. Mopping and dabbing, she had the place in chaos for several minutes, before they had privacy and a fresh pot of coffee.

'You poor girl, you didn't think that Rick and I were still sleeping together, did you?' she demanded bluntly. When Marissa nodded mutely, she clapped a hand to her forehead and groaned. 'Oh, how ghastly that must have been for you! Marissa, I promise you, we're just close, good friends, from way back! Rick was a tower of strength when I needed one, and we were just two busy, lonely people who answered a need in each other. I guess it was more comfort than passion, even then.'

Marissa sat stirring her coffee mechanically, staring at Helena as if she had just revealed a miracle to her. Rick was not being unfaithful to her, either before or during their marriage, and he was not in love with Helena.

'Why didn't I have more faith in him? Why did I ever get that stupid idea in my head?' she mused faintly.

'Because you love him, goose, and love screws up

your logical thought processes,' Helena exclaimed forthrightly. 'I'd lay odds that he loves you too, although he might not have realised it. I never saw him this obsessive about a woman, not even Danuta. *Do* something, Marissa, before it's too late! You musn't allow a misunderstanding to ruin what you two had.'

Marissa sighed.

'It wasn't only that. He thought I had someone else, although I didn't. I loved him too much to endure his not loving me. Oh, it's all too complicated!'

'Then simplify it,' Helena urged briskly. 'Cut the Gordian knot. Talk to him. What have you to lose? Things could hardly be worse than they are—could they?'

Marissa went home to her flat, deep in concentrated thought, seeing neither the streets, her fellow passengers on the tube, or the darkening afternoon around her. She made a pot of tea, drew the curtains, and switched on the gas fire, then sat on the rug in front of it, absent-mindedly warming her hands before the imaginary flames.

There was still a lot she did not understand about Rick. He'd married her for reasons unconnected with love, yet gone out of his way to give her what he thought would make her happy. He'd held her at arm's length, emotionally, but their bodies had made nonsense of the embargo. He'd forbidden possessiveness, but his towering rage when he thought she had betrayed him had surely not all been on account of outraged pride. She had been wrong about him on one very important point—his friendship with Helena. Could she have been mistaken on others?

Helena thought he loved her, and *she* looked at him with eyes unclouded by emotion. Could it be that he *did* care, at least a little, or could learn to? Did they have something that could be salvaged, after all? She, at least, had plenty of love to give—if only he wanted to take it.

'Don't phone him through his lawyers,' Helena had suggested. 'They'll have advised him not to talk to you, and will only put you off. I'll give you Jan's number—both he and Rick are in England now. I know Jan will want to help.'

Rick's brother was guarded but sympathetic when she phoned him.

'Helena said you wanted to talk, but I don't know…you hurt him badly, Marissa. These days I hardly recognise the Rick I used to know.'

Her heart leapt. If that were true, he must have some feeling for her.

'He hurt me too,' she said. 'I just want to meet him, once more. If nothing comes of it, then I promise to leave him alone and let the lawyers get on with their job.'

There was a pause, then Jan said, 'Leave it with me. I can't promise anything, but I'll see what I can do.'

All that day, and the next, she heard nothing, and was beginning to draw the conclusion that Rick had turned down flat any idea of seeing her again. Her hopes turned to lead inside her, for if he spurned this tentative approach, she knew it really had to be all over. She would have to go on without ever knowing whether they might have stood a chance.

Well, she supposed she had her answer, she thought dully. If there had been even a spark of love, Rick would not have refused so emphatically to hear what she had to say.

It snowed a little that morning, a frosty carpet of crystals that turned to slush as Marissa came home from doing a little shopping. She took off her soft leather boots in the hall, and let herself into the living-room, still holding them aloft in her hand.

And looked up to see him standing motionless, back

to the fire, hands clasped behind him, his face neither harsh nor welcoming, but displaying a watchful, waiting expression which made his eyes wary

She gasped.

'Rick! However did you get in here?' she demanded stupidly.

'You shouldn't leave your key under the plant stand in the hall, Marissa. Every burglar in the land knows that old dodge. I'm surprised you haven't been turned over long ago.' he said. The sound of his voice almost brought tears to her eyes, and she wondered how she could live unless she heard it every day of her life.

She dropped the boots, left them spreading a widening puddle on the carpet, and restrained a crazy impulse to rush across the room and fling her arms around him.

'Would you—would you like some coffee?'

'No.' He shifted his stance impatiently. 'Jan said you wanted to talk. I didn't think we had anything to say outside the courts, but he seemed to think I should hear you out. So I'm listening.'

She shook her head wryly.

'You don't make it very easy.'

'It isn't easy. Our last encounter was not pleasant.'

'Not for me either!' she flashed back quickly, then sighed. 'Oh, Rick. I just wanted to say what I should have said then, but didn't, because I was too proud and too angry. I'm sorry about that wretched photograph of me in the nightclub, and all the bother it caused for you.' She licked dry lips, took a deep breath. 'I know what I did was silly, but there really was nothing more to it than what happened on the dance floor. I didn't go to bed with that young man—he wasn't my lover, in fact, I'd never met him before that evening. I didn't…don't…have any lovers, and never have had any, apart from the one I told you about, when I was very young. And you, of course.'

she added lamely.

She sank into a chair, suddenly wearied by the confession, and terribly afraid that it was not making any impact on him. The only reaction she divined was a slight relaxation of the guarded expression in his eyes.

'So that's it? What you brought me here to say?' he demanded, apparently unmoved.

Marissa sighed.

'Yes. Do you believe me?'

'I might,' he said stonily, 'if you could make me understand *why* you ran off to London and indulged in such infantile behaviour, after having moved out of our bedroom and deciding you didn't want to sleep with me any more. Why you rejected me, in fact. It all adds up to a picture of a woman unhappy with her marriage—a woman who knows she's made a mistake, and wants out.'

This was the point of no return. She either told him honestly, and without demur, or let him go, still nursing all his misapprehensions.

'I did all that because…because I was jealous,' she plunged in boldly. 'I got it into my head that you and Helena were lovers…that she was the woman you'd once wanted to marry. I didn't know, then, about you and her sister. You'd never talked about Helena, or invited her to our wedding, but you were so thrilled to see her, so close and happy with her…' She looked down at the carpet, unable to meet his eyes.

And edge of incredulity deepened Rick's voice as he said, 'I didn't invite her to our wedding precisely because she was visiting with Danuta, and they were out in the Australian outback somewhere, uncontactable. Marissa, I have a good many friends you still haven't met, because you simply didn't know me long enough. Of course I was pleased to see Helena. I've known her since we were children, and we've seen each other through many a rough patch. Maybe that's why I didn't talk about her; she's just Helena. I take her for granted, as she does me.'

She heard him move, and suddenly felt the pervasive warmth and male scent of his body as he dropped to one knee at her side.

'Marissa, look at me. I took our marriage very seriously,' he said. She raised her head, pushing back the tumbling dark hair, and gazing into eyes that were all at once intently searching.

'That word you just used—why?' he interrogated sharply. 'You said you were jealous, but why should it have mattered to you what I did? You had what you wanted, what you married me for. You had Grafton Court.'

'Maybe it started out that way,' she said, so softly she was almost whispering. 'But it wasn't enough. When we were in Provence...well, you must remember how it was. And it wasn't "only sex", not for me, Rick. I don't give myself that completely, that easily! Although I know you warned me not to get involved.'

His hand had hers, now, holding it in a crushing grip. 'And did you?'

'Yes. I'm sorry, Rick. I know it wasn't in the agreement, but I ...I fell in love with you.'

Now she had said it, and strangely enough, she did not feel ashamed or stupid, but elated and immensely relieved, as if she had unloaded a great weight from her back.

He rocked back on his heels, laughing softly.

'She's sorry—sorry, she says!' he echoed. And then he seized her, pulling her out of the chair, wrapping his arms round her until they lay on the rug in front of the fire, close and enfolded in one another.

'Marissa, that warning was for my own benefit. I was

trying to keep you at a distance, to prevent *me* from getting too involved,' he muttered raggedly into her hair. 'Don't you know that I had to have you in my life, from the first day I saw you walking Idris, when you threatened to turn a gun on me? But you were determined to see me as the bad guy, so I had to be devious.'

Somehow Marissa struggled free, half sat up, staring down into his face.

'I thought you wanted a hostess—someone to organise your social life! That's what you led me to think,' she accused.

'I could have hired someone to do that! Damn it, I didn't have to surrender my freedom and marry her!' he exploded. 'But you were so obsessed with that house, and the only way to get you was to take on both of you!'

A sudden smile, like sunlight after rain clouds, brightened the lovely face looking down at him.

'Rick Jablonski!' Are you telling me that you love me?' she demanded, with mock severity. 'If so, why don't you get on with it?'

The swiftness with which he changed position, pinning her to the ground, left her breathless, even before he claimed her mouth with his. The world began to dissolve around her, and she wanted, once again, to know the fierce sweetness and delight of him making love to her.

'No—wait,' he said, releasing her lips before the time to say anything sensible had passed. 'I want to tell you something about myself. I grew up hard and rough, because I had to, a lot of the time I'm alone, and yes, I keep things to myself, buttoned up tight. The only woman I'd cared about, before I met you, turned me down, and I was determined not to repeat that experience.

'When I met you, I knew I had to have you, somehow,

that I couldn't turn my back on you and walk away, even though I was afraid you would never really care for me. Perhaps I didn't dare let myself recognise the emotion I felt for you. To you, I admitted nothing. To myself, I called it a lot of things…infatuation, lust, sheer bloody craziness. I simply never called it love, because I didn't know. I do now. I love you, Marissa. What do you want me to do about it?'

Her smile deepened, shining out from the widened tawny eyes.

'Do? Why, Rick, I want you to love me and go on loving me. I want you to take me back as your wife, and go home with me to Grafton Court…so that I can have our baby in the Cottage Hospital, with Dr Pritchard in attendance,' she said softly.

'Holy smoke!' he exclaimed, sitting up, staring at her unbelievingly. 'You're going to have…you *are*? Why the hell didn't you tell me all this the minute you walked in? We could have cut out all this hassle! *My* wife will have *my* child in our home—no question about it!'

Marissa was laughing as she slid her arms round him again.

'I didn't want you to come back to me just because I'm pregnant,' she said. 'I couldn't live with you on those terms, baby or no baby. I wanted a man who loved *me*.'

'Well, you sure as hell have him now,' Rick declared firmly. Marissa closed her eyes contentedly as she rested her head on his shoulder.

I sure as hell do, she thought.

PASSPORT TO ROMANCE VACATION SWEEPSTAKES

OFFICIAL RULES

SWEEPSTAKES RULES AND REGULATIONS. NO PURCHASE NECESSARY.

HOW TO ENTER:

1. To enter, complete this official entry form and return with your invoice in the envelope provided, or print your name, address, telephone number and age on a plain piece of paper and mail to: Passport to Romance, P.O. Box #1397, Buffalo, N.Y. 14269-1397. No mechanically reproduced entries accepted.

2. All entries must be received by the Contest Closing Date, midnight, December 31, 1990 to be eligible.

3. Prizes: There will be ten (10) Grand Prizes awarded, each consisting of a choice of a trip for two people to: i) London, England (approximate retail value $5,050 U.S.); ii) England, Wales and Scotland (approximate retail value $6,400 U.S.); iii) Caribbean Cruise (approximate retail value $7,300 U.S.); iv) Hawaii (approximate retail value $ 9,550 U.S.); v) Greek Island Cruise in the Mediterranean (approximate retail value $12,250 U.S.); vi) France (approximate retail value $7,300 U.S.).

4. Any winner may choose to receive any trip or a cash alternative prize of $5,000.00 U.S. in lieu of the trip.

5. Odds of winning depend on number of entries received.

6. A random draw will be made by Nielsen Promotion Services, an independent judging organization on January 29, 1991, in Buffalo, N.Y., at 11:30 a.m. from all eligible entries received on or before the Contest Closing Date. Any Canadian entrants who are selected must correctly answer a time-limited, mathematical skill-testing question in order to win. Quebec residents may submit any litigation respecting the conduct and awarding of a prize in this contest to the Régie des loteries et courses du Quebec.

7. Full contest rules may be obtained by sending a stamped, self-addressed envelope to: "Passport to Romance Rules Request", P.O. Box 9998, Saint John, New Brunswick, E2L 4N4.

8. Payment of taxes other than air and hotel taxes is the sole responsibility of the winner.

9. Void where prohibited by law.

PASSPORT TO ROMANCE VACATION SWEEPSTAKES

OFFICIAL RULES

SWEEPSTAKES RULES AND REGULATIONS. NO PURCHASE NECESSARY.

HOW TO ENTER:

1. To enter, complete this official entry form and return with your invoice in the envelope provided, or print your name, address, telephone number and age on a plain piece of paper and mail to: Passport to Romance, P.O. Box #1397, Buffalo, N.Y. 14269-1397. No mechanically reproduced entries accepted.

2. All entries must be received by the Contest Closing Date, midnight, December 31, 1990 to be eligible.

3. Prizes: There will be ten (10) Grand Prizes awarded, each consisting of a choice of a trip for two people to: i) London, England (approximate retail value $5,050 U.S.); ii) England, Wales and Scotland (approximate retail value $6,400 U.S.); iii) Caribbean Cruise (approximate retail value $7,300 U.S.); iv) Hawaii (approximate retail value $ 9,550 U.S.); v) Greek Island Cruise in the Mediterranean (approximate retail value $12,250 U.S.); vi) France (approximate retail value $7,300 U.S.).

4. Any winner may choose to receive any trip or a cash alternative prize of $5,000.00 U.S. in lieu of the trip.

5. Odds of winning depend on number of entries received.

6. A random draw will be made by Nielsen Promotion Services, an independent judging organization on January 29, 1991, in Buffalo, N.Y., at 11:30 a.m. from all eligible entries received on or before the Contest Closing Date. Any Canadian entrants who are selected must correctly answer a time-limited, mathematical skill-testing question in order to win. Quebec residents may submit any litigation respecting the conduct and awarding of a prize in this contest to the Régie des loteries et courses du Quebec.

7. Full contest rules may be obtained by sending a stamped, self-addressed envelope to: "Passport to Romance Rules Request", P.O. Box 9998, Saint John, New Brunswick, E2L 4N4.

8. Payment of taxes other than air and hotel taxes is the sole responsibility of the winner.

9. Void where prohibited by law.

VACATION SWEEPSTAKES

Official Entry Form

Yes, enter me in the drawing for one of ten Vacations-for-Two! If I'm a winner, I'll get my choice of any of the six different destinations being offered — and I won't have to decide until after I'm notified!

Return entries with invoice in envelope provided along with Daily Travel Allowance Voucher. Each book in your shipment has two entry forms — and the more you enter, the better your chance of winning!

Name _____

Address _____ Apt. _____

City _____ State/Prov. _____ Zip/Postal Code _____

Daytime phone number _____
                                    Area Code

☐ I am enclosing a Daily Travel
   Allowance Voucher in the amount of **$**_____ Write in amount
                                    revealed beneath scratch-off

© 1990 HARLEQUIN ENTERPRISES LTD.

VACATION SWEEPSTAKES

MONTH 3 ENTRY

Official Entry Form

Yes, enter me in the drawing for one of ten Vacations-for-Two! If I'm a winner, I'll get my choice of any of the six different destinations being offered — and I won't have to decide until after I'm notified!

Return entries with invoice in envelope provided along with Daily Travel Allowance Voucher. Each book in your shipment has two entry forms — and the more you enter, the better your chance of winning!

Name _____

Address _____ Apt. _____

City _____ State/Prov. _____ Zip/Postal Code _____

Daytime phone number _____
                                    Area Code

☐ I am enclosing a Daily Travel
   Allowance Voucher in the amount of **$**_____ Write in amount
                                    revealed beneath scratch-off

CPS-THREE